DEAD BY DESIGN

DEAD BY DESIGN

ANISH SARKAR

An imprint of Manjul Publishing House Pvt. Ltd.
• C-16, Sector 3, Noida, Uttar Pradesh 201 301, India
Website: www.manjulindia.com

Registered Office:
• 2nd Floor, Usha Preet Complex, 42 Malviya Nagar,
Bhopal 462 003 – India

Distribution Centres
Ahmedabad, Bengaluru, Chennai, Hyderabad,
Kochi, Kolkata, Mumbai, Noida, Pune

Dead by Design by Anish Sarkar

This paperback edition first published in India in 2025

ISBN 978-93-5543-972-7

Cover Design: Wasim Helal

To the Good Wife

1

When Dev Malik woke up that day, he had no idea that he had only a short while left to live.

The screen of his mobile phone showed 5.15 a.m., well before the time his alarm had been set. All those years of late nights and irregular work schedules had disrupted his body clock for good. Further sleep was impossible. He got out of bed and padded over to the bathroom.

The face that stared back at him in the mirror, with its square jaw, broad forehead and dark, brooding eyes, was strikingly handsome. Dev didn't like the fact that his thick mop of wavy hair was greying at the sides, but it made him even more irresistible to women. And men too, if they were so inclined.

Despite minimal exercise, his body remained strong and lean. It was the natural robustness of his Punjabi genes. Dev knew it wouldn't last much longer though, for he was already in his mid-thirties. He had recently made a concession by signing up for a yoga class but quickly realised that he had no patience for any of the asanas.

His trusty manservant, who had been with the family for almost four decades, had gone to Raigarh for his annual vacation. So Dev brewed himself a cup of his favourite Darjeeling blend sourced from a renowned tea taster, and walked out onto the expansive balcony.

Dev's apartment was on the thirty-second floor overlooking the Worli promenade, with a spectacular view of the Arabian Sea. The Maximum City was still asleep, with sunrise an hour away. The only people visible were a pair of joggers, a woman walking her dog, and a policeman leaning against his parked van. The lights of the moored fishing boats and cargo ships could be seen in the distance. Dev knew the peace and quiet would soon be broken by the dawn of another bustling day in the great metropolis.

He rustled up a breakfast of scrambled eggs on toast and fired up the Nespresso machine as he ate. Dev had been living alone for a while now and was an adept-enough cook. Besides, one was anyway spoiled for choice with all the food-delivery platforms. He took his coffee to the study and switched on his MacBook.

He was due to have lunch with the founder of an HR tech start-up at the Bombay Gymkhana Club and opened the pitch deck for another look. The financial projections were impossibly ambitious, but that wasn't a problem for Dev because he knew it came with the territory. These days, one couldn't be a tech entrepreneur and not want to rule the world.

It used to be so different in my time, thought Dev.

Dev's grandfather, Balram, had arrived in Ludhiana after Partition as a homeless migrant from the erstwhile West Punjab. He had no money, but the capacity for enterprise and hard work ran strong in his veins. After trying his hand at different small businesses, none of which took off, he finally set up a hotel in the city, one of the first commercial properties. As the city industrialised in the 1950s, his hotel flourished with the government becoming one of its prime patrons. In a few years, Balram opened a second hotel, a bigger and grander one.

However, his only son, Dev's father, had no interest in running a hospitality business and was bent on joining the military. Balram sold his hotels for a neat profit and he moved to New Delhi, where he built a large bungalow and a small hosiery shop in Rajouri Garden. His son, meantime, enrolled in the Indian Navy and went on to become a Vice Admiral in the Western Naval Command in Mumbai.

Dev was born at INS Ashwini in Colaba. He was a cherubic and friendly child, early signs of the immense charm that would come later. When he was nine years old, his father sent him to the Lawrence School in Sanawar, known not only for its reputation as an elite boarding school but also for its military traditions and alumni. Dev enjoyed the next seven years amidst the idyllic Kasauli hills but showed little interest in joining the armed forces, much to his father's disappointment.

In fact, Dev had already figured out that he wanted to be an entrepreneur. Balram, who doted on his grandson, was suitably pleased and promised to fund Dev's venture but only after he completed his graduation. There were a couple of initial failures, which Balram didn't mind for he hadn't forgotten his own days of struggle in Ludhiana.

It was 2009, and the world was slowly getting back on its feet after the worst financial crisis in nearly a century. E-commerce was starting to pick up even in India, and the seeds of the next wave of internet-based start-ups were being sown. Dev was advised by his then-girlfriend, a consultant with McKinsey, to get into online retailing, which she predicted was going to disrupt the world in the coming decade. He took the advice seriously, even if not the relationship.

Dev's first step was to create a website for selling clothes, leveraging the supply chain and inventory of Balram's shop in Delhi, which had become a mini department store by that time. Back then, however, people were not comfortable buying garments without trying them on. Other sites were mainly selling books, music and gift items. Dev realised that he needed to think of something else.

He hit upon the idea of selling electronic products online, an outcome of some market research but mostly gut instinct. Using all his persuasion skills, he managed to convince two major electronics manufacturers, one domestic and the other South Korean, to open up a channel to sell directly to consumers using his website. It was surprisingly successful. Within eighteen months, Dev had a hundred brands on his platform, employed a team of ninety people, and was doing over a thousand transactions a month.

It was a heady time. Dev was working fourteen hours a day, seven days a week, but he didn't mind. It was worth the excitement of seeing his company grow much faster than he had ever imagined, and profitably too. He raised funds from a venture-capital firm, much against Balram's wishes, who warned him that he risked losing control.

As it turned out, Dev's business began to slow down after a couple of years. The competition had intensified, global funding was gushing in, and commissions were getting squeezed by original equipment manufacturers and their distributors. But the new mantra was scale, not margins. Dev had the most coveted asset, a large, loyal consumer base, and his investors brokered a lucrative deal to sell out to one of the cash-rich marketplaces.

Dev walked away with a cool $15 million.

Digital and social technologies had completely transformed the landscape since Dev's days as an entrepreneur, but the basics hadn't changed—you still needed a great idea, a passionate team and a working capital runway.

He was excited to get back into the game, so to speak, except that he was now a coach rather than a player. The technology-led innovation that was happening in the country was breathtaking. His own street credentials as one of the early success stories of e-commerce meant that many start-ups were keen on his association, especially in any advisory or operational capacity. That was not for him though, and he spent his energies picking the right ones to invest in, usually passively.

Dev decided to go to the Bombay Gymkhana a little early. After a long shower, he changed into chinos and a linen shirt, paired with a corduroy jacket. It was January and even though Mumbai hardly had any winter to boast of, the weather was unusually cool. He drove out in his gleaming Jaguar XF sedan, for which he had recently traded in his ageing BMW. It almost felt patriotic, since the iconic British car manufacturer was now owned by the Tatas.

He sat at his usual table on the long veranda of the club, sipping on a gin and tonic. A cricket match was in progress on the verdant grounds in front, probably between two rival club teams. Dev had never taken much interest in cricket, preferring football and tennis.

When his guest arrived, Dev was surprised at how young he was. It ended up being a long lunch, for he wanted to understand the business model better, and more importantly, assess how committed the founder really was. Dev noticed a spark in the boy and finally made up his mind to not only put in an investment but make it a bigger ticket size than usual.

It was past four o'clock by the time Dev got back home. His part-time maid had come in and cleaned the apartment in his absence. She usually stayed until dinner, but he had asked her to leave early that day. He had had one drink too many, and thought of brewing himself a coffee but eventually decided to sleep it off.

The evening would be a long one and Dev was really looking forward to it. He had plans to cook dinner himself and fixed on a fusion menu of shammi kebabs, lemon butter fish, a simple pasta, and focaccia. The preparation was done—the lamb mince marinated for twenty-four hours, the choicest beckti delivered all the way from Versova, and the penne kept parboiled. Only the ice cream remained to be ordered in.

After his siesta, Dev luxuriated in his home jacuzzi for a while before taking a second shower. He then slipped into his favourite outfit of black tee and blue jeans, of which there were at least fifteen sets in his wardrobe. At home, he was always barefoot, for he loved the feel of the marble floor.

By eight-thirty, everything was ready. The drawing room was suffused with the soft glow of Turkish mosaic ceiling lights and an antique stand lamp bought from a store in Kochi. A bottle of Alsace Riesling (he preferred the French one to the German), and a Tuscan Chianti were chilling in the fridge. His impressive collection of single malts and other spirits gleamed in the backlit bar.

Dev sat on the slightly worn leather sofa and closed his eyes, listening to the soothing jazz of Miles Davis playing on his Harman Kardon home theatre. As he waited, he thought about all the effort he had just put in. It was quite unlike him, and it wasn't as if it was a special day or anything like that. However, he felt happier than he had in months.

The doorbell rang just then, as expected. Dev opened the door, but his welcoming smile turned into a look of surprise.

2

Sharon Sequeira woke up at exactly the same time as Dev that morning. She had always been an early riser and didn't need any alarm.

Her four-year-old son was sleeping next to her, one little arm curled around her neck. He had his own room but would invariably get up in the middle of the night and come to her bed. She gently pushed him away and kissed his forehead. Everyone said he looked like her. He had her eyes, complexion and hair, though the gummy smile was definitely inherited from his father. Sharon sighed at the memory of her late husband.

It was a chilly morning, and the streetlight just outside her window was shrouded in mist, which was unusual. She shivered, wrapping the duvet closer around herself. A strange sense of foreboding swept through her. She checked her messages, and there was the usual mix of forwards, late-night arguments on her college group, a couple of appointment reminders and the customary good morning image from her driver who had recently discovered WhatsApp.

Sharon shrugged off her lethargy and got out of bed. Something continued to bother her, but she couldn't put a finger to it. She walked over to her mother's room to check on her, as she did first thing every morning. Mrs Sequeira was a spry sixty-eight, but she had sleep apnea and needed to put on a special device every night to regulate her breathing. Sharon found her fast asleep, snoring gently.

She changed into her tracks and threw on a sweatshirt. Having sworn off caffeine some months ago, she made herself a cup of green tea with a dash of honey. When a nutritionist explained to Sharon how commercial honey was made, she was appalled. All the processing done to give it the artificially smooth and transparent texture actually killed the nutrients, and most producers put in sugar and other additives to further dilute the original extract. She had immediately switched to raw honey which was far more expensive but worth the premium.

By six o' clock, Sharon was out of the door, wheeling along her bicycle. It was a top-of-the-range Avon Dakota 21-speed model which cost almost as much as a second-hand scooter. While researching her options, she figured out that when it came to two-wheelers, be it motorcycles, scooters, or bicycles, India was the manufacturing hub of the world. She finally decided on Avon, the seventy-year-old company that had made millions of Indians mobile.

It was dark outside and the streets were deserted, except for the odd morning walker or milkman. Mumbai wouldn't wake up before another hour at least. Sharon didn't feel scared though, for the city was relatively safe for women. Had it been Delhi, it would have been a very different matter. Besides, she had a brown belt in taekwondo and felt confident of defending herself, if it came to that.

Once, when Sharon was walking back home from a friend's house late at night, she sensed a man following her. She quickened her pace, and he did the same. Her house was still several minutes away. Since she was wearing heels, it would be impossible to make a run for it anyway. So, she suddenly turned around and began walking towards him.

The man stopped in his tracks, surprised. Sharon saw that he was around her height, and stocky. His face wasn't clearly visible, but she guessed he was in his early thirties. She went right up to him and wagged a long finger in his face. 'Are you following me?'

He leered at her. 'Yeah, baby. Why don't you come… with me? We can… have some fun.' His breath stank of cheap liquor.

In response, Sharon gave him a resounding slap and then punched him twice in the solar plexus. The man doubled over, shocked by the unexpected attack. Sidestepping, she kicked him expertly in the knees. He collapsed into a heap this time, groaning. Sharon kicked him again in the side, just hard enough to crack a rib.

'Don't ever do that again, you bastard. Be thankful I didn't kill you!' She walked off without looking back.

Sharon parked her cycle outside Joggers Park and walked in. It was right at the intersection of Turner Road and

Carter Road, and the plaque at the entrance read 'From Sir with Love'. It was a tribute to a veteran hockey coach who developed the park by transforming a dumping ground that had stood at the site.

There used to be a small entrance fee charged earlier, but that has stopped. With its beautiful location right by the sea, Joggers Park attracted large crowds in the evenings. People came to watch the sunset and enjoy the breeze more than for any real exercise. In the mornings though, it was generally the serious fitness enthusiasts who would be found walking or jogging on its two concentric tracks.

Sharon completed her ten-kilometre run in fifty minutes and monitored her falling pulse rate on her Fitbit. She could easily complete a half marathon, but her aim was to participate in a full one. She had given herself a year to prepare for it. An upcoming Bollywood actor, who lived in Bandra and was also a regular at the park, smiled at her as he jogged past. She ignored him. *He is probably used to girls falling all over him*, she thought, *but I'm not part of that groupie brigade.*

The sun was up by the time Sharon got back home. She saw an unmarked, brown envelope next to the newspaper on the mat outside the front door. She picked both up and was about to open the envelope when her son burst out and hugged her tightly. Laughing, she picked him up but held him away from her, his legs kicking furiously.

'Mama's all sweaty, sweetheart.'

The boy pouted. 'You're never there when I wake up.'

She put him down. 'Come on, let's check on Granny.'

They went in, and Sharon threw the unopened envelope on top of a pile of old papers next to the shoe cabinet. She figured it was some useless promotional material.

After a quick shower, Sharon had a whey protein shake and a bowl of dry fruits. It was part of the strict diet she was on. She only indulged herself during the weekends, that too for any one meal in the day, usually breakfast. However, that evening would be an exception, and she was looking forward to it.

Her phone rang on cue and she smiled.

'Good morning, baby.' The voice sounded deeper than usual.

'Mmm, you sound sexy in the mornings.'

He chuckled. 'That's what all the girls tell me.'

'Not any more they don't, you lecherous man.'

Deftly changing the topic, he asked, 'So how was your run this morning?'

'Oh, the usual. But I still need to do a lot of work on my stamina.'

'I could help you there.'

'We'll see about that tonight. But I have to first take care of all my patients. The diary's packed today.'

'All work and no play…'

'Yeah, but you know that's me. Anyway, see you in the evening, darling.'

'Can't wait.'

Sharon sighed as she hung up. She never thought it would feel so good to be hopelessly in love. But she had never felt so insanely possessive either.

Dev had always been a ladies' man. His first sexual encounter was with a buxom widow who worked as the manager in Balram's shop. Dev was spending his summer holidays with his grandfather and was all of fifteen years old. She had come to the house one afternoon to drop off some papers, and Dev was alone at home. He was already a tall and strapping lad by then and had proudly grown his first moustache. One thing led to another, and they ended up on the large sofa in the drawing room, throwing caution to the wind.

There had been no looking back for Dev after that. At eighteen, he was already on his fifth girlfriend. By the time he finished college, he lost count of his one-night stands. In his mid-twenties, he was an established and compulsive womaniser. 'He can't keep his dick in his pants,' was the common refrain among anyone who knew Dev well.

The fact was that Dev was devilishly attractive to a wide spectrum of women, from teenagers to middle-aged mothers. Not only was he terribly good-looking, but he had a funny yet naughty sense of humour that was irresistible. When he looked deep into a girl's eyes and cracked his slightly crooked smile, it never failed to get her pheromones racing. 'It's not my fault that God made me this way,' he would tell his close buddies, quite seriously.

When Dev sold his e-commerce venture, Balram, who was in the last stages of lung cancer, had insisted that he hire a wealth manager to invest all the money prudently and ensure a comfortable income for the rest of his life. It was the last thing on Dev's mind in the midst of all the euphoria. However, he deeply respected his grandfather and obeyed his wishes but not before splurging on a luxury apartment and a BMW 5 Series sedan.

Balram passed away soon after, and Dev was grief-stricken. His friend, philosopher, and guide had been taken away from him. He realised that he had been closer to his grandfather than to his own parents and Balram had certainly had a far bigger influence on Dev's life than they ever did. Even from his deathbed, Balram had made him take the right decision, for which he would be eternally grateful.

Dev decided to go on a three-month-long trip to Europe. He had visited London a couple of times and stopped over briefly in Amsterdam once. But that was about it. There hadn't been much time to holiday while he was building his start-up. He decided to begin with Spain and Italy and work his way north to Scandinavia. But he never made it that far.

It was July, and the Mediterranean beaches were packed with people from all over the continent. He didn't look out of place and could easily pass off as one of the Spaniards, especially with their summer tans. Language was a problem, but there were enough people who could speak passable English, and Dev was able to strike up conversations with strangers. There were hardly any Indians there at that time of the year, and his stories of tigers and spirituality and Ayurvedic massage were both exotic and fascinating.

The weather was brilliant, with blue skies and endless sunshine. Everyone was in a holiday mood, and ready to have fun all the time. In the first couple of weeks, Dev slept with women from five different countries. There was one incredible night with a pair of Creole twins from Jamaica who were on their first trip to Europe. It was all like a dream. Dev's love life had slowed down over the past few years as he immersed himself in his business, but he was furiously making up for lost time.

On his last night in Venice, a local woman he had met at a bar invited him later to her house by the canal. But a man opened the door when he knocked. Dev made some excuse about the wrong address and ran, without waiting to find out what had happened. It was a sign that he needed a break from the non-stop partying, and he took a flight to Paris the next morning. *Time for some sightseeing in the world's most historic city.*

Over the next three days, Dev soaked in Paris. He walked down the Champs-Élysées, went up to the top of the Eiffel Tower, and sat at the Place de la Concorde. He visited Sacré-Cœur and explored Montmartre, even getting the customary portrait sketched. He spent a full day at the Musée du Louvre and the Musée d'Orsay, and then took a Bateaux Parisiens cruise on the Seine in the evening. All alone, and he thoroughly enjoyed it.

On the fourth day, he met Minnie.

3

As she drove towards her dental clinic, Sharon let her mind wander to the first time she met Dev.

Sharon loved animals, especially horses. She started equestrian lessons when she was eight years old and was an expert by the time she entered her teens. There was a scar on her face caused by a fall from a particularly ill-tempered pony. But it hadn't scared her off riding. The only problem was that once she graduated from cantering to galloping, there weren't any places within Mumbai where there was enough space for it. There were races every week at the Turf Club, but that was for professional jockeys only.

Sharon finally discovered a ranch an hour from the city that had an extensive riding course and a stable that included a pair of sleek Kathiawaris with their characteristic, inward-curved ears. On most weekends, she would drive up and spend a couple of relaxed and blissful hours there. There was nothing more exhilarating than riding a fine horse. It was like flying.

The ranch also had a shelter which took in and rehabilitated old, injured, sick, or abandoned animals. The owner, a sixty-three-year-old Anglo-Indian widow, had rescued over a couple of hundred dogs, cats, goats, ponies, ducks, hens and cows. Sharon invariably spent some time with the animals after her riding was done. Her favourite was a frisky street dog which had lost a leg in an accident but still jumped around on the remaining three with great energy.

One day, as Sharon completed her final circuit and took the horse towards its stable, she noticed the ranch owner standing there with the most gorgeous man she had seen in a long time. She took off her helmet and looked down at herself, wishing she wasn't so dishevelled and sweaty.

'Sharon, meet Dev Malik,' the woman said brightly. 'My late husband and Dev's father were colleagues in the navy. I've been trying to get him to visit the farm for a long time.'

Dev smiled, making her go weak in the knees. 'Nice to meet you, Sharon.'

She dismounted and held out her hand. 'Hi, Dev.' His grip was firm, almost intimate.

The woman turned to Dev and said, 'Sharon's a regular here, you know. By the way, she's a dentist. So if you ever have any tooth trouble, you know where to go.'

Dev laughed, showing a set of perfect teeth. *He won't ever need to see the inside of a dentist's chamber*, Sharon thought ruefully. *How unfortunate.*

The ranch owner asked her to join them for lunch. But Sharon was reluctant, for she desperately needed a shower and a change of clothes. Dev was clearly keen for her to stay on, and said, 'Don't go, Sharon. You'll be missing out on the best shepherd's pie in the world.'

That wasn't what Sharon was worried about missing out on. It had been ages since she socialised with a man, let alone someone as attractive as Dev. There was nothing more she would have liked than to spend more time with him, but she didn't want to make a poor first impression either.

The woman realised her predicament, and said, 'You can freshen up in my house, dear. I think I may have a dress of my daughter's that should fit you nicely.'

The lunch went on until late afternoon. After they finished dessert, a delicious cheesecake, the woman excused herself, saying she needed to go for her siesta. She had also brought out some home-made limoncello for the two of them. Sharon and Dev decided to go for a walk around the ranch, carrying the bottle and two glasses. There was a stream flowing right along the property, and they sat down on a grassy patch next to it.

It was almost dusk by the time they got back to the house. Sharon was tipsy after having drunk too much limoncello, and her sides ached from all the laughter. Dev was as charming and funny as he was good-looking, and it had been an incredibly fun afternoon. More than once, she felt this strong urge to kiss him but restrained herself. *Not that it looked like he would have minded.*

That night, Sharon couldn't get Dev out of her mind. She was pretty sure he was attracted to her too, though it was impossible to believe that a man like that didn't have other women in his life. Every time she had tried to probe his relationship status, Dev had deftly changed the topic. It was only the next morning that she did some research on him, and figured out that not only was Dev married but also an established womaniser. However, Sharon was totally smitten with him by then.

Sharon parked her car and entered the clinic with thoughts of Dev still floating in her mind. There were two Japanese men waiting for her at the small reception.

She had bought a state-of-the-art 3D dental imaging machine, and it was delivered the previous day. Unlike conventional X-rays, 3D imaging provided a complete view of the patient's oral and dental anatomy with exceptional clarity.

Seeing Sharon, the men stood up and bowed. They were formally dressed with smart ties and gleaming shoes. She saw the logo of the dental equipment manufacturer on their white shirts and concluded that they had come to install the new machine. The company had set up their operations in India recently and was largely staffed by expats.

An hour later, it was done. *This will be a game-changer for my practice,* Sharon thought, marvelling at how innovative the new technology was. The machine was almost the size of a piano, but it was easy to use. All that the patient had to do was stand still for a few seconds, holding two handles and biting down on a sanitised mouthpiece. Her guinea pig was a particularly difficult but loyal patient, and he was happy to get something free for a change.

After a busy morning, Sharon decided to step out for lunch instead of having the sandwich her mother had packed. It was a cool, clear day, and Candies was just a ten-minute walk from the clinic. The Reclamation outlet was smaller than the original place, which was spread over three floors of a converted house, but it had the same assortment of fresh, ready meals and delicious desserts.

Sharon ignored the tempting displays inside the glass counters and chose a salad. Candies was packed as usual, so she took her tray and found an empty table under the awning outside. It was one of those rare days in Mumbai when one could enjoy the weather without any air conditioning. Even the flies had disappeared.

She had just started to eat when her phone buzzed. It was an unsaved number, but Sharon rarely ignored such calls because nine times out of ten, it would be a patient. She preferred to be more reachable than most other dentists.

'Hello?'

'Sharon Sequeira?' It was a woman, the voice sounding muffled as if her mouth was covered.

'Yes, it is. Who is this?'

'I left something for you this morning. Did you see it?'

'What? Where?'

'A brown envelope. At your house.'

Sharon remembered. 'I… No. Who are you?'

'Never mind. Call me back when you see it.'

'Wait…' But the woman had already hung up.

Sharon was puzzled. The voice sounded vaguely familiar, though it was obviously not one of her patients. She called home, but no one answered. She guessed her mother had gone to the bus stop to pick up her son after school. She looked at her watch. It was already getting late for her afternoon appointments so she quickly finished her lunch and walked back to the clinic.

The woman called Sharon again after a couple of hours, this time on the board line at the clinic. She was completing an extraction procedure when her assistant came in and whispered, 'Someone's on the line for you. She says it's a matter of life and death.'

Sharon asked one of the junior dentists to take over and went to her office. Closing the door behind her, she picked up the desk phone.

'Why aren't you taking my calls?' It was the same voice.

Sharon looked at her mobile, which was in silent mode. There were several missed calls from the same number.

'I was with a patient.' She was angry now. 'Who the hell are you? And what do you want?'

'I'm just a well-wisher.'

'Why are you calling me?'

There was a pause. 'Sharon, I have information that you really need to know.'

'Information about what?'

'Not what. Whom.'

'All right, whom then?' She sounded exasperated.

'Your beloved boyfriend.'

Sharon felt like she had been kicked in the stomach. She couldn't speak for a couple of moments.

'Hello? You there, Sharon?'

'Yes… I…'

'It's not too late. You can still get out of it.'

'What... do you mean?'

'I mean, you know he can't stay away from women, right?'

'He's... totally faithful to me.'

The woman laughed. 'Are you sure?'

Sharon composed herself. 'Look, I don't want to discuss this. Stop bothering me!'

'All right. But go home and take a look at what's inside that envelope. I have a feeling you'll want to speak to me again after that.'

'Why can't you tell me what's in it?'

'I wouldn't want to spoil the surprise, darling. Call me. Let's meet this evening. I'll tell you everything.'

Sharon slammed the phone down.

She called in her assistant and told her to cancel the remaining appointments for the day. Quickly finishing up some pending paperwork, she left for home.

Mrs Sequeira was surprised to see her daughter back early.

'Everything okay, dear?'

'Yes, Ma. I had forgotten something.' She stared at the empty space next to the shoe cabinet. 'Where are the papers that were here?'

'The kabadiwala had come. I gave them to him.'

Sharon clenched her teeth. 'Shit!'

'What happened? It was just some old newspapers.'

'Was there a brown envelope in the pile?'

'No, I'm pretty sure there wasn't.' Mrs Sequeira thought for a moment. 'Wait, I think I saw my grandson drawing on something... Maybe...'

Without waiting for her mother to finish, Sharon went to her son's room. Sure enough, there was the envelope on his bed, doodled over with crayons but still sealed. She picked it up and slit open the flap with a fingernail.

Three enlarged photographs spilled out. The resolution wasn't great, but the two people in them were unmistakable. Sharon closed her eyes and sat down on the bed.

She felt an uncontrollable fury rise inside her.

4

DCP Kabir Khan of the Mumbai Crime Branch sat in his spartan office at the Crawford Market headquarters. He always came to work by eight o'clock in the morning, much before anyone else.

Kabir was checking emails on an ancient desktop and eating a *Parsi* omelette delivered from a nearby Irani cafe when his mobile phone rang. It was the commissioner. He was surprised because she rarely called that early.

Kabir wiped his mouth and took the call. 'Good morning, ma'am.'

'Morning, Kabir.' She sounded tense. 'Have you seen the news?'

He thought for a moment and asked, 'You mean the murder in Worli last night?'

'Yes. Dev Malik.' She paused. 'I knew him well.'

'I see.' He wondered what the connection was but waited for her to go on.

'I want you to handle the case, Kabir.' She generally didn't waste words.

'Certainly, ma'am.'

'I've already spoken to Patil from Worli thana. He will brief you.' She hung up.

The Crime Branch investigated serious crimes only, a small fraction of the FIRs registered in the city every year. It wasn't unusual for them to be roped in quickly into a case, especially when the victim was high-profile and media attention was likely. This one had already been picked up by news channels. Besides, the commissioner herself had headed the elite unit a few years back and probably trusted them to do a better job than the local cops, given her own personal connection to the case.

The Crime Branch has traditionally been the jewel in the crown of the Mumbai Police. Its notable successes included the arrest of India's most infamous serial killer Raman Raghav, the capture of the notorious Charles Sobhraj, and the uncovering of the conspiracy behind the 1993 bomb blasts within a few hours. In the 1990s, officers of the Crime Branch and their constables had built excellent networks of informants throughout the city, and by the turn of the millennium, broke the back of the storeyed Mumbai underworld by arresting hundreds of gangsters working for all the major dons.

However, two decades on, the nature of crime in the city had changed dramatically. The Mumbai mafia could never get back to their heydays from the 1980s and all the erstwhile gang bosses were either in jail or had gone into hiding in different countries. Cyber fraud, economic offences, drug-running and sexual crimes took centre stage, not to mention cross-border terrorism.

In this transformed landscape, the Crime Branch lost some of its past glory. The new cadre of officers struggled to emulate the success of their predecessors and were often dogged by controversies. Nevertheless, they were still at their best when handed a good, old-fashioned murder to solve.

Kabir set out immediately on his Royal Enfield Bullet 500. He could have used a police van driven by one of the constables but generally preferred to move around on his motorcycle. He loved the deep, staccato thumping of the powerful engine as he sped on the concrete roads of the island city, the light bar and siren cleaving the rush-hour traffic.

He reached the Worli police station in fifteen minutes flat and walked into the familiar white-and-red building. Senior Inspector Harish Patil, whom he had messaged just before leaving, was there to receive him. He saluted Kabir, and the two men shook hands warmly. They had worked together on a couple of cases in the past, a burglary-cum-murder and a rape of a foreigner, and not only cracked both but in the process, developed a strong regard for each other.

'Good morning, Harish.'

'Good morning, sir. Please come in.'

'Harish, how many times have I told you not to call me "sir"?' Kabir put his hand on the shoulder of the other man, who only smiled back.

They sat on beige moulded-plastic chairs in an anteroom next to Patil's chamber, sipping on kadak chai from paper cups. The physical contrast between the two could not have been starker. Kabir was tall and swarthy, with a strong but wiry frame. His hair was flecked with grey and thinning at the top. Patil, on the other hand, was of average height and plump. He sported a paunch that should not have been allowed on an active policeman. Despite being in his early fifties, he had a headful of dark, curly hair.

The two men had vastly different backgrounds as well. Harish Patil was born to the family of a poor farmer in a village called Vadgaon, near the holy city of Nashik. He studied in the local primary school until the age of fourteen and then travelled to Mumbai to find work. At his father's behest, a man from the same village, who worked as a cook in a Kurla restaurant, offered him temporary lodging in his tiny tenement in Dharavi.

Patil started out washing dishes in the same restaurant and tried various odd jobs before finding employment as a full-time house help with an old couple who lived alone in a bungalow in Dadar. In the midst of all the cooking, washing and cleaning, and with the encouragement and funding from his new benefactors, he managed to complete his education and even secured a graduate degree through a correspondence course.

He joined the Mumbai Police as a trainee and coincidentally, his first posting was at the Worli thana. He slowly rose through the ranks, building up the reputation of a solid, hard-working policeman with a lot of courage. After stints in the Anti-Terrorist Squad and the Narcotics Cell, which helped him to learn new investigation tools and expand his skills in detection, Patil was promoted to the rank of Senior Inspector and eventually given charge of the station where he had started his career all those years ago.

Kabir's parents were both criminal lawyers and had built up a successful practice together, litigating cases in the Bombay High Court. He grew up in a huge apartment on Woodhouse Road in Colaba and studied at the elite Cathedral and John Connon School. An above-average student, young Kabir was nevertheless far more interested in sports, representing the school in both cricket and football, a rare feat. Despite his parents' cajoling, he had no interest in pursuing a career in law and settled on a degree in commerce from Sydenham College.

After completing his graduation, Kabir began interning at an accounting firm owned by a family friend but realised in a few months that it wasn't for him. By then, he had started to develop a strong yearning to join the police force. It was only natural, for Kabir had been exposed to the world of crime from an early age through glimpses into his parents' profession.

They weren't happy with his career choice, but Kabir had always been headstrong. He sat at home and prepared hard for the UPSC examination, which he cleared with flying colours the following year. In fact, his rank was good enough for selection to the IAS or the IFS, which his father implored him to join instead, pointing out how prestigious both services were and the great work he could be doing. However, Kabir was hell-bent on the IPS.

The first year was at the National Police Academy in Hyderabad, where Kabir was trained in weapons, physical combat, Indian laws, police procedures and so on. His inaugural posting as ASP was in Gadchiroli, the easternmost district of his home state, which would later become a feared battleground of the Maoist movement.

While experiencing police work at the grassroots level, Kabir got practical lessons in understanding the criminal mind, collecting evidence, extracting confessions, dealing with courts, and navigating societal dynamics.

After a second posting in the interiors, this time in drought-prone Beed, Kabir was assigned to the traffic wing in Mumbai. While it was good to be back home, the work was mostly administrative, and he hated it. When he heard about an opening for a deputation with the Central Bureau of Investigation—the CBI—in Delhi, he applied for it and got selected. The next three years were exhilarating for Kabir, as he worked on the worst crimes in the country with its best investigative sleuths. At the end of it, he returned to Mumbai and joined the Crime Branch, which is where he had always wanted to be.

'Dev Malik,' Patil began. 'Son of a senior naval officer, he made his wealth by selling his internet company some years ago. Since then, he has lived the life of a rich socialite, enjoying all the luxuries money can buy. Oh, and he has apparently slept with half the women of south Mumbai, sir.'

Kabir knew some of this. He had already googled the victim. 'And his wife is a television actress, right?'

'Yes, that's correct. She calls herself Tanya B and is quite a celebrity. She played the lead role in one of the popular, long-running soaps on TV and was the winner in a reality show last year. That's what really made her a household name. But she's been estranged from Dev for some months now and lives separately.' He smiled and added, 'I'm a fan of hers, sir.'

'Walk me through exactly what happened last night, Harish.'

'At 10.30 p.m., there was a call on the twenty-four-hour police helpline from the Ocean West apartment complex, saying that one of the residents had been killed. A beat marshal who was in the area, and a mobile van stationed at the Worli Sea Face, rushed to the building, sir.'

Patil paused for a moment and continued, 'Around half an hour before we got the call, a food-delivery guy had come with an order of ice cream to Dev's apartment, and the security guard in the lobby dialled up on the intercom, but no one answered. As per protocol, the guard then accompanied the boy up to the thirty-second floor and waited as he rang the doorbell. They tried several times, but the door wasn't opened.

'The guard was certain Dev was home and panicked. He banged on the door of the apartment opposite, which coincidentally happened to belong to the current chairman of the society. He's a retired corporate executive and he came out immediately, having already heard the agitated voices in the landing.

'The chairman first tried calling Dev's mobile, but there was no response, even though they could hear it ringing inside the apartment. Then, they decided to break open his front door and stumbled inside. They found Dev lying in a pool of blood on the carpet in his drawing room.'

Patil sighed. 'The man was quite dead.'

5

A constable came into the room and placed a plate of kanda bhajiya on the desk. Kabir helped himself to a couple, and asked, 'Do we have a time of death?'

Patil shook his head. 'Not yet, sir, but the victim hadn't been dead for long when they found him. He had been stabbed three times, twice in the stomach and once in the chest.'

'What happened after that?'

'One of them dialled 100, I don't know who, and as I mentioned earlier, we had people nearby who responded immediately. As soon as I was informed, I rounded up my sub-inspector and a few constables and reached there. After collecting basic evidence and sealing the apartment, we interrogated the security guard and the delivery boy, who told us the sequence of events. The society chairman, who was naturally shaken, had nothing to offer on what might have happened. He did, however, have the number of Dev's dad, and I called him right away, sir.

'Vice Admiral Malik, the father, arrived soon after getting the news. He's a widower and was devastated to see his son lying dead, but as befits a military man I suppose, he recovered his composure. We shifted the victim's body to JJ Hospital for post-mortem, and I got the Forensic Science Laboratory—the FSL—to send one of their men to help my team in forensics. They've been there since early morning, sir.'

'What about the wife? Didn't you call her?'

'I asked Dev's father, but he didn't want to right then and said he would break the news to her later. I got the impression he didn't care much for her. Anyway, she's there at the apartment now, and we'll be questioning her today.'

'Did anyone else visit Dev that evening?'

Patil smirked. 'Ah, now we come to the interesting part, sir. According to the security guard, a woman came to Dev's apartment at 8.45 p.m. and was there for an hour before leaving. He claimed that she was his "girlfriend", and a regular visitor, so much so that he didn't even bother to ask her to sign the register. He did dial Dev on the intercom though, who asked her to be allowed up. We looked at the CCTV recording, and it corroborated his statement.'

'Do we know the identity of this woman?'

'Yes. Her name is Sharon Sequeira, sir. She's a doctor, a dentist actually, and has her own practice in Bandra. It looks like Dev has been seeing her for a few months now, according to a couple of neighbours we spoke to. This lady is a widow, by the way, and lives with her mother and four-year-old son. The guard said that she would usually stay much longer at Dev's place, often until the next morning. But that day, she left surprisingly early. In the CCTV footage from the lobby, she looks quite agitated and walks out hurriedly.'

'So we have our main suspect then?'

'Yes sir, in all likelihood. We have no evidence right now that anyone else visited Dev that evening. He had gone out for lunch to the Bombay Gymkhana and returned in the afternoon. He has a part-time maid, who came in, cleaned the apartment and left. An old manservant lives with him, but he's presently away at his native place.

'It seems like Dev was expecting Ms Sequeira for dinner, sir. The dining table was set for two people, a glass of wine and a tumbler of whisky lay unfinished next to the sofa, and there was music playing in the drawing room. Looks like they had some kind of a fight that escalated suddenly, ending in the woman stabbing him to death.'

'Did you find the murder weapon?'

'No, sir. However, we think it could be one of the kitchen knives because one is missing from the stand.'

'And you say the neighbours heard nothing, no noise or shouting while all this was going on?'

'Nothing at all. But remember sir, this is a luxury complex, and soundproofing is bound to be good since the rich like their privacy.'

'Do you have the suspect in custody yet?'

'That's the thing, sir. We obtained her mobile number and tried calling from the victim's apartment itself, but it was switched off. Then I called the duty officer at Khar thana and asked him to dispatch a couple of constables to her place in Union Park. Her mother told them that

Sharon hadn't been home all evening. We issued a missing person alert immediately, and informed all the major hospitals as well.'

Patil rubbed his forehead. 'Unfortunately, there's still no sign of Ms Sequeira. It seems like she's disappeared.'

Tanya sat on the sofa and stared blankly at the pool of dried blood on the carpet. She imagined Dev lying there lifeless, a knife stuck in him. The smell of death lingered in the room. The forensics team had left a short while ago, and she was alone.

With no make-up and her hair tied in a bun, Tanya looked very different from her public image as a TV star. She was in a pair of faded jeans and a simple cotton shirt with rolled-up sleeves. Her large spectacles, which she rarely wore outside her own home, couldn't hide the fact that her eyes were red and swollen.

The doorbell rang with its familiar chime, and she got up to open the door. Two men stood outside. They were obviously police officers, though only one of them was in uniform.

The taller man, who was dressed in grey and black, said, 'I'm DCP Kabir Khan from the Crime Branch, and this is Senior Inspector Harish Patil from the Worli thana. May we come in?'

'Yes, of course.' They followed her inside.

'We're very sorry for your loss, ma'am,' said Patil.

She nodded and said, 'I was going to make some coffee. Can I offer you gentlemen some?'

'Yes, thank you.'

A little later, the three of them sat at the dining table with their cups.

'This is a terrible shock,' Tanya began. 'Dev and I were separated, and we've lived apart for a while. He had many faults, but I can't imagine anyone wanting to kill him.'

Kabir asked, 'When did you last see him?'

She thought for a moment. 'Actually, just a week ago. He wanted to discuss our divorce and asked me to come to our… this apartment. It was the first time either of us had brought it up. We had loved each other deeply, you know, and thought… hoped that the separation would perhaps bring us back together.'

She choked and looked away.

'Don't worry, ma'am,' Patil said. 'We can speak later if you want.' He had an infatuated look on his face, and Kabir glared at him.

After a moment, Tanya said, 'I'm okay. Please go on.'

Kabir took out a Dictaphone and switched it on. He said firmly, 'I'll need to record this conversation if you don't mind.'

She looked at him sharply. 'Am I a suspect?'

'Just routine procedure, ma'am,' Kabir continued smoothly. 'When did you last speak to Dev?'

'He called me up the day before yesterday. We were to meet next week with our respective counsels and plan the next steps. It was quite amicable actually. We had finally agreed that it was time to move on. Money wasn't a problem, since I earned enough and didn't want alimony. We don't have any children either.'

'Did he sound worried about anything?'

'Not at all. He spoke about his work, bitched about lawyers' fees, cracked a couple of jokes... It was just Dev being himself.'

'Was he working? I thought he didn't need to.'

'You're right. Dev was rich and also managed his money well. His latest passion was getting back into the start-up world through angel investing. That's what he was talking about.'

Patil piped up. 'Do you know a Sharon Sequeira, ma'am?'

Tanya's face hardened. She said tersely, 'She's Dev's latest squeeze. I haven't met her myself.'

'How did you find out?'

'It's common knowledge now. Many of my friends have seen them together.' She sneered. 'Since it's lasted more than a couple of months, I can only assume that Dev was more serious about her than his usual flings.'

The two men looked at each other. Then Kabir said, 'We think Ms Sequeira might have killed your husband, ma'am.'

6

It was a gloomy afternoon in Paris, with the summer sun having decided to take a break. Minnie had stepped out of her hotel in tracks and a sweatshirt, planning to have a run along the banks of the Seine, but the weather played spoilsport.

The drizzle forced her to seek shelter in a cafe. As she took a table and ordered a cappuccino, she noticed a man sitting by the window. He was very handsome and probably Indian, but she couldn't be sure. He looked up from the book he was reading and checked her out, a tad longer than was necessary.

Minnie decided to ignore him. She took out her mobile phone and immersed herself in it. Just then, the skies broke and it began to rain heavily. She looked up and grimaced. The man by the window, who had been casting covert glances at her, seemed to take a cue. Without getting up, he asked her, 'Hi, are you from India?'

She stared at him for a moment, debating whether to answer and finally said, 'Yes, from Delhi. And you?'

'Mumbai.' He flashed a dazzling smile. 'The rain is unexpected, huh?'

She looked outside and made a face. 'Yeah, and this is supposed to be summer.'

'How long have you been here?'

'I only arrived yesterday. It's my first trip to Paris.'

'Mine too.' He took his coffee and walked over to her table. 'May I?'

This time, she didn't hesitate. Pointing to an empty chair, she said, 'Please do.'

He put out a hand and said rather formally, 'Dev.'

His hand felt warm and strong. 'Minnie.'

'Minnie... As in the little girl from Tagore's *Kabuliwala*?' He smiled again, disarmingly.

'Yes,' she replied. A shadow seemed to pass over her face.

After a pause, Minnie asked, 'What about you, Dev? Where are you from?'

'Well, my roots are in Punjab but on the Pakistan side, from where my grandfather came to India as a refugee during Partition. My dad was in the navy though, so I've grown up in different places.'

'I see. And you're here on holiday or work?'

'I'm on a holiday,' he said, adding, 'alone.'

'Me too.'

Dev grinned. 'And now we're both stuck here, aren't we?'

Minnie was born in a planter's bungalow at a tea estate near Dibrugarh. The premier Assam Medical College and Hospital was less than fifty kilometres away, but her mother had gone into labour suddenly and her father, the estate manager, who was on his early morning rounds of the plantation, couldn't be contacted. Under the able supervision of onc of the older tea-pickers, who had played midwife for many deliveries in the tribal community, there was a happy outcome, which often wasn't the case in the tea gardens. The healthy, brown newborn, curled in her mother's lap, was named Minnie by her father.

Assam is the world's largest tea-growing region and accounts for more than half of India's production. The British had set up the first tea plantations in Assam in the 1830s, after a Scottish explorer Robert Bruce, who was on a trading mission, apparently found the tea plant *Camellia Sinensis* growing wild in the state. The rich clay soil of the lowlands on either side of the Brahmaputra River, and the climate, with its cool winters and long, wet monsoons, made perfect conditions for growing tea. By the 1860s, the business had grown rapidly, with over 150 tea gardens established in the region.

Minnie's father worked for one of the erstwhile British tea companies that had sold out to a prominent Marwari family of Kolkata in the 1960s. Until then, the tea industry and its way of life had been firmly rooted in the traditions of the Raj. For well over a century, the tea gardens had been managed by British planters who ruled like demi-gods over the tribal labourers. They lived in sprawling bungalows, attended to by a retinue of servants, spent their evenings at the planter's clubs, and played golf on the weekends.

When Minnie was growing up, vestiges of that lifestyle still remained. The bungalow they lived in, dating back to the nineteenth century, was built on stilts, and its rooms had high ceilings and period furniture. The culture of gastronomy hadn't diminished either, with an ample supply of fresh vegetables and fruits grown at home and everything else flown in from Calcutta. The bar at the Dibrugarh District Planters' Club continued to draw its old patrons on Saturday evenings, and boasted of a functional, 18-hole golf course, even as many other courses in the state were reclaimed by weeds.

Minnie was an extremely intelligent child. Her Assamese mother, who came from a humble background, had high ambitions for her elder daughter, who doted on her in return. She sent Minnie to study in an elite Catholic school in Kolkata at the age of ten, while the younger one remained with her in the tea gardens. Minnie lived with her grandparents for a couple of years before her father got transferred back to the company head office in the city. She was a star student in the school and went on to top the board exams. Her mother wanted Minnie to apply to colleges abroad for her graduation, but Minnie ended up enrolling at St. Stephen's in Delhi. Though she loved her mother dearly, Minnie was clear that she didn't want to leave the country just yet.

By then, Minnie had become a striking young woman. She was tall and slim, with the long limbs of an athlete, and had the alluring hazel eyes of her mother which looked even more exotic against the dusky skin inherited from her father. Minnie wasn't classically beautiful, for her mouth was too wide, her chin a tad aggressive, and her nose slightly mishappen from a fall in her childhood. But she never failed to turn heads, of both men and women alike.

Minnie developed a strong interest in theatre and joined the Shakespeare Society, one of the oldest and most venerated fraternities at Stephen's. She was also a regular participant in student fashion shows, being much in demand for her model-like figure. In her final year, a talent scout for an advertising firm spotted her at a college fest and offered a role in a TV commercial for a popular beverage company. The ad was highly successful, with Minnie's youthful and charming face becoming an instant hit with viewers.

The downside of this new-found fame became quickly apparent. Whenever she went out anywhere, she was subjected to stares, catcalls and even the odd grope. It was all too much for Minnie. She knew she had to get away, and accepted an admission offer from the prestigious Columbia University in the US for her master's degree, finally fulfilling her mother's wishes in the bargain.

Fate had other plans, though. Six months later, Minnie received the news that her mother had committed suicide.

As Kabir finished narrating the sequence of events pieced together by the police, Tanya exclaimed, 'That bloody bitch!'

She put her head in her hands and started crying.

Kabir got up and fetched a box of tissues he had spotted on the bar cabinet. Tanya took a couple and wiped her eyes.

'Thank you,' she mumbled. 'Dev... had cooked for her... last night. I saw the food in... the fridge. All his signature dishes. He must have been serious about... that woman. How could she do this to him?'

Patil said, 'We'll find Ms Sequeira and bring her to justice, ma'am.'

'That slut should be tried and hanged in public. No other punishment can ever be good enough…' Her voice rose in a crescendo.

Kabir said gently, 'Look, I can't even imagine how upsetting this must be for you. We'll just ask you a few more questions and then leave.'

Without waiting for a response, he continued, 'Do you live alone now, ma'am?'

Tanya nodded. 'After we separated, I moved to my apartment in Parel.'

'Where were you last night between eight and ten?'

She looked hurt. 'So you *do* think I'm a suspect? Even after everything you told me.'

'Ma'am, it's our job to investigate all the facts thoroughly.'

'Well, if you must know, I was at home all evening.' She paused. 'And not that it should matter, but Jeet was at my place.'

'Jeet, the singer?'

'Yes.'

Patil had filled in Kabir on the rumours about Tanya having an affair with the ageing but influential doyen of Hindi film music. Jeet, who only went by that single name, was both a singer and a composer, having many hits to his credit over the years. He was one of the judges in the show Tanya had won. He was known to have a roving eye and had been openly appreciative of her, almost downright biased, right through the competition.

Born in Guwahati, Jeet started his career as a popular Assamese folk singer, until he got noticed by a famous

Bollywood actor–producer who wanted a different genre of music for his upcoming period film. There was no looking back for him after that. He shifted to Mumbai and quickly made a name for himself, as much for his distinctive, rasping voice as for his versatile range of compositions.

'Are you romantically involved with him?'

'I don't think I need to answer that question.' Her tone was defiant.

Kabir said quietly, 'We'll have to speak to him anyway.'

'I... we... have nothing to hide.'

Patil asked, 'Ma'am, is there anything else you want to tell us, anything that you think can help in this case?'

'No.' She abruptly got up. 'I think we're done here.'

7

'WHAT did you think of her, sir?' Patil asked, as soon as they got into his Bolero.

Kabir smiled. 'Well, you seemed very impressed, Harish.'

'No, no, sir,' he replied, looking sheepish. 'I… It was just that she was so upset.'

'Don't forget that Tanya is an actress by profession.'

Patil stared at him. 'Do you think she was lying, sir?'

'No, I'm not saying that.' Kabir looked thoughtful. 'I can't put my finger to it, but something tells me this case isn't as simple as it looks.'

'We'll investigate every detail, of course.'

'The first thing is to find Sharon Sequeira quickly, Harish.'

'At the moment, our assumption has to be that after murdering Dev in a fit of rage, she realised the enormity of what she's done and has gone into hiding somewhere.'

Something struck Kabir. 'Did she drive to Dev's building in her own car last night?'

'Yes, she did, sir. We checked the security register at the gate, and her car number was noted there. The time of entry at 8.40 p.m. It's a Honda Jazz, and she was at the wheel.'

'That doesn't sound like a well-to-do dentist's car.'

'She also has a Skoda Superb with a chauffeur but preferred the smaller Jazz when she drove herself, sir.'

'Did the security guards at the main gate speak to her?'

'She just waved from inside the car and drove right through. Since she's a familiar visitor, they let her go.'

'Is her face visible in the CCTV footage?'

'Not clearly, sir.'

'All right, let's see what we can find out from her mother.'

They got off the Sea Link towards Bandra and drove through Turner Road onto the promenade, passing an old fishing village before turning into Khar Danda. After a few minutes, Patil stopped in front of a dilapidated three-storey building in a leafy lane.

'This is it,' he announced.

They walked up to the second floor and rang the doorbell. A woman of about sixty-five opened the door, an unwelcoming look on her face.

Kabir said, 'Mrs Sequeira? I'm DCP Kabir Khan and this is SI Patil. Can we please come in?'

She stood aside without saying anything, and the two policemen walked in.

The apartment was quite different from the shabby exterior. The walls looked freshly painted and the granite flooring was clearly expensive. The furniture in the living room was an eclectic mix of antique wooden pieces, brightly coloured sofas, a painted trunk for a centre table and a modern floor-to-ceiling showcase. It was quite dark inside though, as all the houses were cheek by jowl, something no interior decorator could fix.

Kabir noticed a large framed photo of a woman in riding gear and boots, standing next to a magnificent black horse. From the rolling fields and gabled houses in the background, he guessed that it was clicked somewhere in Europe. It was undoubtedly Sharon Sequeira. She had a dusky complexion, large eyes and thick, curly hair like her mother but was taller. Her face was attractive in a Halle Berry kind of way, except for a distinctive, white scar that ran from the corner of her right eye and down the cheek. She had the fit, athletic look of someone who loved the outdoors.

'Please sit down,' said Mrs Sequeira.

'We're investigating the murder of Dev Malik,' Patil began. 'I believe your daughter Sharon knew him?'

'Officer, the Khar police visited me last night and also this morning. So I know why you're here. Yes, my daughter knew that man, but she has absolutely nothing to do with his death. Do you understand?' Her voice was tense and defiant.

Kabir said calmly, 'Ma'am, we're sorry to inconvenience you. However, a very serious crime has been committed, and we have reason to believe that Ms Sequeira was at the victim's place last night. So we really need to ask you a few questions.'

'All right, if you must.' She sniffed. 'Your friends have already asked me all the questions, but no one has any answers for where my daughter has gone.'

'When did you last see her?'

'Sharon left home at around six, saying she was going to be out for dinner. I didn't ask where, though she did tell me that she would be back at night. My grandson called her around nine to ask about something, but her phone was switched off, which was unlike her. We tried again after some time, and that's when I started to worry.'

'Are you sure she left home at six? That's a little early for dinner, isn't it?'

'Yes, I'm sure,' she said with some asperity. 'Sharon's normally at her clinic until well past seven but returned by five last evening.'

'Did she appear upset or disturbed in any way?'

Mrs Sequeira thought for a moment. 'Not really, but she was very quiet. I just assumed something was on her mind. She changed and left without having tea with me, as she usually does.'

'What was she wearing, by the way?'

'Uh, let me see. It was a red dress.' She suddenly started to cry. 'Sharon looked... so pretty in it. When... will... my daughter come back, officer?'

Patil chimed in, 'We've issued a bulletin across all our units to keep a lookout for her, ma'am. I hope we find her soon.'

'Do you think... she could have had... an accident?'

'I don't think so, ma'am. The hospitals have been alerted, and we would have known if she was admitted anywhere last night.' Patil cleared his throat. 'It's possible she may be deliberately hiding. Can you think of any place she could have gone?'

Mrs Sequeira wiped her tears and glared at him. 'I know my daughter, inspector. She's the most open and honest person you can imagine. Even if she's done anything wrong, which she certainly hasn't, she'll never hide because of it.'

Patil pressed on. 'Can you tell us about your daughter's relationship with Dev Malik, ma'am?'

'I feel… really tired. I can't answer… any more questions. Please…' She looked beseechingly at both men.

Kabir nodded to Patil and stood up. 'No problem, ma'am. We can come back later.'

As they were leaving, Mrs Sequeira said, 'You should… speak to Rhea. She's Sharon's childhood friend.'

Rhea Menon had first met Sharon at Villa Theresa when the two six-year-olds were assigned seats next to each other in class. It turned out that they had more in common. Not only had Rhea's father just moved from Dubai and taken up a job in the engineering company where Sharon's father worked as a finance manager, but he had also rented an apartment in the same lane where the Sequeira's ancestral home stood. The families got acquainted in due course, but it was the two girls who became inseparable as they were growing up.

After graduating from high school, they decided to choose different paths. Sharon had always wanted to be a doctor, but she baulked at the long and difficult MBBS course, not to mention the tough preparation for all the entrance tests. Her uncle was a dentist, and he advised her that it was much easier to become one. He also predicted that dental technology was developing fast and with more and more Indians being able to afford speciality treatment, it would soon become a lucrative profession. Sharon took his advice and did well enough in the CBSE-administered test to gain admission to a venerated dental college in south Mumbai.

Rhea wasn't quite as focused and cleared her boards with only average marks. She managed to get into a middle-rung college in Mumbai University, that too through the waitlist. The next three years would be a struggle for her academically, but Rhea became a popular student, with girls and boys alike. She was petite and pixie-faced and had an infectious laugh. Everyone loved her warmth and energy.

Rhea fell in love with a senior in the very first year of college. Everyone called him Bala, even though he had a much longer name. Bala was quiet and geeky and ambitious, everything Rhea was not. He wasn't happy studying in what he considered an inferior institution and was determined to do better for himself. His goal was an MBA, and from his second year, he had started preparations for the CAT, escaping to the library whenever he could. That's where he first met Rhea.

It was as clichéd as it could get. Rhea couldn't find the book on medieval history she was looking for. Bala was the only other student around, and she asked him to help. He not only located the book for her but also offered to share his old notes, which he boasted were perfect for last-minute cramming. Rhea's gratitude turned to affection, and the unlikely duo soon became a known couple on campus.

Bala's CAT score wasn't as good as he had hoped for, but it got him into a decent-enough business school in Delhi. Rhea joined an advertising agency as a client-servicing associate, where her sociable personality stood her in good stead. But after Bala got placed at a coveted multinational, she chucked her job and they got married. Within a year, they were parents to twin girls.

Through all these years, Sharon and Rhea remained in close touch, following each other's lives with interest. Sharon had done the one-year mandatory internship at her uncle's dental clinic in Pune and continued there after graduation. She was a quick learner, and in three years, decided to return to Mumbai and set up her own practice. Her uncle advised her that it was too early, but she went ahead regardless, making a sensible move by hiring a more experienced but less enterprising dentist to assist her.

Sharon's love life was less successful. She had an on-off boyfriend in college, but there had been no time for serious romance. Spurred on by Rhea, she went out on a couple of blind dates, and later ended up having a brief, torrid fling with a much-married newspaper editor. It ended badly, and Sharon swore off any commitments with men.

Then one day, a shy but attractive patient came to her with a root canal problem. The routine procedure was completed in one sitting, yet he kept coming back with some complaint or the other until she had to tell him that his teeth were in perfect condition. He blurted out that all he wanted was to ask her out to dinner, and though surprised, Sharon found herself accepting. *I don't mind staring at his salt-and-pepper hair for an evening*, she thought to herself.

His name was Jai Prakash Singh, and he was quite a bit older than Sharon. JP, as he was known, had started as a hotel management trainee with a luxury hotel chain and went on to become the executive chef at one of its iconic properties. He then quit his job of sixteen years and set up an eponymous fusion bistro in a converted villa on Carter Road, aided by funding from two angel investors.

Though *Jaypee's* was a popular restaurant, Sharon hadn't been there before and was glad for it. JP pulled out all the stops to impress her, closing the place to the public for the evening and laying out a spectacular menu paired with the best wines in the house. In his own den, JP was a different person, charming and funny, even romantic.

Sharon was swept off her feet, and they were married in six months.

Rhea was in a state of shock. She had seen the news of Dev's death on TV in the morning and called Sharon immediately, but her phone was switched off. Then the messages started to come in. *Sharon's the prime suspect, and she's missing.*

The previous afternoon, Rhea was out walking her two pugs when Sharon had called.

'Ri?'

'Hey babe, what's up?'

'Can't hear you properly. Where are you?'

Rhea was at Bandstand, and the strong sea breeze was whistling through the connection.

'I'll be home in ten minutes. Can I call you back then?'

There was silence at the other end. Rhea asked, 'Shar, you there?'

'Listen, I really need to talk.'

Sensing something in Sharon's tone, Rhea quickly crossed the road and sat down at an outdoor table of the neighbourhood coffee shop, where it was a little less noisy. She said, 'Okay, tell me.'

'Ri, I got a call just now from a stranger, a woman. She said she has very important information about Dev that I need to know.'

'Oh, and what was the information?'

'She wants to meet me... Didn't say much on the phone, except implying that Dev is cheating on me.'

'What's her name?'

'She didn't say.'

'Hmm, very mysterious...' Rhea paused. 'Are you sure it isn't someone pranking you?'

'I'm not sure.' Sharon sounded hesitant. 'But I doubt it somehow.'

'So you're going to meet her?'

'I... suppose so. She said something weird like, "It's a matter of life and death."'

Rhea didn't respond for a moment.

Sharon asked, 'What could she have meant?'

'Maybe she's an ex of Dev's, out to spite him. God knows there are so many.'

'That's what I thought as well.'

'How's it going between Dev and you?'

Sharon's voice lightened up. 'Never been better, touch wood. I really think we're in love. He's cooking dinner for me at his place tonight.'

'How romantic,' Rhea said drily. She had never approved of Dev, knowing his reputation only too well. 'Then Shar, why are you bothered by this woman? Just ignore her.'

After a pause, Sharon replied, 'I need to find out what she has to say. What if... she really knows something?'

'Don't go. I... suddenly have a bad feeling about this.'

'I'll be fine, don't worry. Bye, Ri.' She hung up.

Rhea felt a wave of guilt and panic rise inside her.

8

HARIBHAI 'Harry' Shah was a worried man.

Harry lived in the Ocean West complex, his apartment the one right below Dev's. It belonged to a family friend from Bristol, who had bought it as an investment in the heydays of Mumbai's real estate boom. Empty all these years, the owner was happy to be finally renting it out to an acquaintance.

Harry was born in Nairobi, but his family had moved to England when he was very young. They were British passport holders already and owned a wholesale retailing business in Kenya. His father decided that London wasn't the place to be, and chose the quieter Bristol to live in. Building on his experience from Africa, he set up one of the largest grocery stores catering to the small but growing South Asian community in the city.

As a child, Harry was quite average, showing no particular aptitude or talent. His father had hoped that his firstborn would be able to inherit and grow the business, but it wasn't to be. Harry demonstrated little interest in trading or enterprise and instead developed an early desire for all things expensive, much to his parents' ire. He became friends with a group of rich kids in school, who set the benchmark for him with their lavish clothes, beautiful mansions and fancy cars.

Harry's father was reasonably well-off but certainly not in that league. He prospered steadily over the years, opening up two more stores, and foraying into the lucrative spice-trading business. At heart though, he remained a conservative and thrifty Gujarati, and while they moved into a larger house, their lifestyle was by no means extravagant. Harry's feelings of deprivation only grew, made worse by his complete lack of accomplishment in academics, sports, or any other field of activity. By the time he turned eighteen, he was already a disillusioned young man, convinced that life had given him short shrift.

His father felt that Harry needed a change to shake him up, and sent him to India for his graduation. He paid what he considered a princely sum of money to get his son admitted into a newly established private college that welcomed NRIs without regard to any aptitude or qualification. Harry protested mightily, for though the family went to India every other year, he felt no connection with the country of his forefathers at all.

His father stood firm in his decision, and Harry found himself on an Air India flight to Delhi with a one-way ticket. He struggled in the initial weeks. His Hindi was poor, and everyone made fun of his British accent. He had little idea of local customs and manners, or indeed, of the realities of urban life in India. Then, a senior who lived in the same dorm noticed Harry's plight and decided to take him under his wing. He had also spotted something else in Harry, but that would be for later.

This new friend happened to be the general secretary of the fledgling student union in the college and was a dubious character. He taught Harry that every problem had a solution, even if not fully legitimate. Any rule could be broken, usually in ways that could be hidden. And there were many ways to make easy money, none of them legal. This particularly appealed to the impressionable Harry, who had always longed to be rich.

One evening, after the two of them had finished discussing a plan to open a betting syndicate in college for the upcoming cricket World Cup, one thing led to another and Harry discovered a new fact about himself.

He was gay.

When the doorbell rang the previous night, Harry was sitting on his balcony with a glass of rum in his hand. He had first developed a taste for Old Monk in college and rediscovered it recently after many years. Whenever he was tense, which was often these days, he found that it worked even better than weed in calming him.

He went over to the front door and looked through the peephole. The sight of a man in khaki unnerved him. He still asked, 'Who is it?'

A gruff voice responded, 'Police. We need to speak to you.'

Harry took a couple of deep breaths and opened the door. Two constables walked in. He nervously asked them to come inside, but they remained in the foyer.

Without any preamble, one of them said, 'Your neighbour upstairs, Dev Malik, has been murdered.'

Harry looked shocked. 'Oh my God!'

'We think it happened maybe between nine and ten this evening. Did you hear any sounds or voices coming from his apartment around that time?'

'I… No… I mean, how…'

'He was stabbed to death,' said the second constable, adding officiously, 'we can't really say anything more at this point.'

'I… was at home but didn't hear anything… at all.'

'Did you know Dev Malik?'

'Not too well… We weren't friends if that's what you're asking.'

'When did you last see him?'

'Uh… L-let me think,' Harry stammered, thinking furiously. 'I guess… we met in the lift… some days back maybe.'

He felt their eyes boring into him but then put it down to the normal bedside manner of policemen everywhere. *They can't possibly be suspicious of me.*

The first constable, obviously the junior one, opened a small notebook and wrote something down. He then looked up and asked, 'Mr Shah, do you know if the deceased had any enemies? Who could have done this to him?'

'I… have no idea, sir.' Harry shook his head. 'May the poor man's soul rest in peace.'

'All right. We may come back later to ask you more questions.'

Harry closed the door behind them and ran to the bathroom where he threw up.

Harry had his first brush with the law when he was twenty-four years old, and was working for a secret poker club in south Mumbai. It was run by a top city lawyer and attracted many high-and-mighty people who were addicted to gambling. The club supposedly had all the requisite licences and was known for its discretion, but it was illegal, of course. Harry's job was to liaise with the patrons, and also get in new clientele. His British accent fitted in well with the exclusive image the owner wanted to cultivate.

Inevitably, the police raided the den one night and arrested everyone they could get their hands on, including Harry. He spent the night locked up in the same cell as a retired Test cricketer and the infamous husband of a noted Bollywood actress. The next morning, they were all let off without any charges, and everything was hushed up. Luckily, even the media hadn't got a whiff of it.

The poker club quietly restarted operations in a different location, but Harry decided to move on. He had made several useful contacts while working there, and one of them was a man who had a thriving business in fake luxury goods.

It was a lucrative and growing market, accounting for over half of the entire global trade in fakes, far ahead of other categories like pharmaceuticals and entertainment products. In India too, the erstwhile trade in smuggled electronics and other 'imported' goods from Thailand and Nepal had rapidly become unviable after liberalisation in the 1990s. Coupled with rising incomes and demand for high-end brands, the focus had started to shift to counterfeit watches, bags and clothes emblazoned with famous logos.

Harry joined the man's business aided in no small measure by the fact that he had also slept with him, something his new boss didn't want the wife to know. The front was a registered company that ostensibly imported speciality yarn and fabrics for textile manufacturers, but what they really imported were fake designer clothes and shoes from China, which made their way to the high-street markets in Delhi and Mumbai.

On his second trip to Shenzhen, Harry discovered that a few counterfeiters were producing fakes in the same factories where the original items were being manufactured, and were quietly pilfering from the bill of materials. In particular, the watches made this way were of outstanding quality and very difficult to differentiate from the genuine ones. Harry convinced his principal that he was on to a good thing, and they soon became a supplier of 'limited edition' imitation luxury watches that dealers would quietly slip in among their legitimate stock.

It was hugely profitable while it lasted. Sadly for Harry, the Swiss companies, whose watches they were ripping off, figured out what was going on, and shut off the illegal trade at its source by clamping down on their outsourced operations in China. Harry tried to replicate the same modus operandi with women's bags and discovered the manufacturing unit of an uber-luxury fashion brand in Guangzhou where they were making excellent fakes with the leftover materials. But it was a cat-and-mouse game, which he realised wasn't going to be sustainable for them.

By then, Harry had insisted on a stake in the firm, which the proprietor had no option but to agree to, even though the two of them were no longer involved physically.

They had expanded into new markets in tier-II cities, where people's aspirations were growing even faster than their wealth, and the duo managed to stay clear of the law through a combination of bribery and luck.

During those years, Harry made a lot of money, but he ended up spending even more. His lifelong dream to be rich was finally realised, and he couldn't handle it, unfortunately. Initially, it was designer clothes, a German car and a duplex apartment, the things he had always felt deprived of. There was a string of boyfriends, on whom Harry lavished expensive gifts. Then, it went on to gambling and betting, spurred by his indefatigable lust to get richer even more quickly.

It went the way it usually does, and Harry was soon deep in debt. He borrowed from friends, embezzled from the company, sold his prized possessions one by one, and yet sank deeper into the hole he had dug for himself. As a last resort, he went to a loan shark with connections to the underworld, but it was a vicious spiral and there was no way he could pay back. The threats began to come, and he was beaten up by goons as he was walking home one evening. Harry knew his life was in serious danger.

There was only one thing to do. He called his father and told him everything. Two days later, he was on a flight to Bristol, leaving everything behind.

Twenty-four hours had gone by since Dev's death, and Harry hadn't slept a wink since then. He feared that the police would come back during the day to question him again, but they didn't. He was sure they would return eventually, though. Thankfully, he was alone at home, having recently broken up with the young architect he had been seeing.

Why did I lie to those two constables? He cursed himself. *I could have at least said something closer to the truth. Now it will look very suspicious when they find out.* He thought of going back to the police himself and spilling the beans but couldn't. Not yet, at least.

In fact, Harry knew Dev much better than he had let on. He had first seen him over a year ago in the building lobby, and his heart missed a beat. Harry hadn't seen a better-looking man in a long time. He made discreet enquiries and learnt more about Dev, including the fact that he was a notorious womaniser. That didn't deter Harry, for he had known many men like that who simply hadn't yet discovered their homosexual side.

Harry was finally introduced to him at a potluck dinner organised by a common neighbour, where Dev was polite but aloof. They bumped into each other off and on after that, at community events in the complex, or in the parking lot where their spots were adjacent, or even in the lift. Harry tried to build up the acquaintance by connecting with him on social media and messaging him occasionally. Then one Sunday evening, he casually invited Dev over to his apartment for a drink saying that he wanted some investment advice.

Dev was in two minds, but he accepted Harry's invitation as a neighbourly gesture. He was wary of the man, having heard several unsavoury rumours about his past but had to admit to himself that he had seemed nice enough in all their interactions. Harry's shaved head (he had kept it that way ever since he began losing hair), medium build and pleasant smile made for a disarming image. Dev, however, had no idea of his host's sexual orientation.

After some desultory conversation, Harry began to ask Dev questions about his personal life, edging closer to him on the sofa they were sitting on. He knew he was coming on too strong, and it wasn't his usual style. But he couldn't help himself. Initially, Dev just found it weird and wondered when Harry would get to the point and bring up the investment he wanted to discuss.

There was no investment, of course. Knowing that Dev loved single malts, Harry had opened up the most expensive bottle in his own collection, a twenty-five-year Bowmore, and they were soon on their second round. Dev had, by then, figured out that there was something wrong with his host but decided to have a final peg of the exquisite whisky before leaving. Harry went to fix it and surreptitiously added a dose of ketamine from the small vial hidden in his bar. It was something he normally used only with young and vulnerable dates, but he went ahead on a crazy impulse anyway.

Unfortunately for him, Dev noticed. Finally realising what the evening was all about, he got up and confronted Harry, punched him in the face and stormed out.

9

Kabir stared at the mynah sitting on the sill outside the single latticed window of his office. *One for sorrow.* An old superstition and it wasn't a good omen.

He turned to Patil and asked, 'Still no sign of Sharon Sequeira?'

'No, sir. We've extended the alert across the state and also in Goa.'

Kabir had his own team in the Crime Branch, but he had requested Patil to continue on the case, hoping to replicate their past success in working together.

'We haven't had any luck with tracking her mobile phone, right?' He helped himself to a handful of besan-coated peanuts and pushed the bowl towards Patil.

'No, thank you, sir. My wife has put me on a strict diet.' Patil gave a sheepish smile. 'Anyway, to answer your question, the last-known location of Ms Sequeira's phone is the victim's apartment. Looks like she not only switched it off there but also took out the battery. In case she switches it on at any time, we'll find out.'

'What about her call records?'

'Her last identifiable call that evening was to a Rhea Menon.' Patil was blessed with a good memory and didn't need to consult any notes. 'They're childhood friends, as Mrs Sequeira told us. She lives in Bandra, and I've sent a couple of my men to question her today.'

'Anything else?'

'We're still checking the list, but they seem to be routine calls. Some patients, her mother, the bank, a neighbourhood grocer and so on. And yes, quite a few to Dev Malik. Looks like they spoke every day, sometimes more than once.'

'That means their relationship was probably going well.' Kabir looked thoughtful. 'So, what would make her kill him suddenly like that?'

Patil didn't reply. It was a rhetorical question anyway. If they knew the answer, the case would have been solved.

A constable came in and handed over a document to Kabir. 'Sir, the post-mortem report of the victim has just come from JJ Hospital.'

'Ah, thank you, Shinde. I was waiting for this.'

He quickly scanned the report with an experienced eye and then passed it to Patil. Thankfully, it was a computer printout. The hand-written reports of the past were often illegible, and created problems for both the police and the courts, especially in medico-legal cases.

Kabir waited patiently as Patil pulled out a slim plastic case from his trouser pocket, extracted a pair of uncharacteristically trendy reading glasses and slowly went through the report word by word. He finally put down the document and declared, 'There doesn't seem to be anything unexpected, sir.'

Kabir shook his head. 'The post-mortem report always has important clues in a murder case. You just have to find them.'

'Sir, the report corroborates the fact that this is a death by stabbing, doesn't it?'

'There are nevertheless a few points to note, Harish. First, the wounds were very deep, indicating that the killer was strong. Maybe exceptionally strong for a woman.'

Patil interjected. 'Sir, Ms Sequeira is tall and athletic. She didn't look weak to me at all.'

'Yes, you could be right.' Kabir paused. 'Besides, anger can lend extra strength to a person, if indeed the crime was committed in anger.'

'The evidence points to that, sir.'

'Does it?' Kabir steepled his fingers under his aquiline nose.

Patil grinned. 'Sir, you look just like Sherlock Holmes in that serial on TV.'

'You watched it, Harish? I'm impressed.' He sounded condescending, without really meaning to be.

'Yes, sir. Isn't he the inspiration for all detectives, real or fictional?'

'Indeed. Anyway, the second finding in the post-mortem that struck me as important is the fact that the final blow of the knife missed the heart and punctured a lung. What does that tell you?'

'I'm not sure, sir.'

'Sharon Sequeira was a doctor. Yes, a dentist but a medical professional nonetheless. Do you think someone like that would not know where exactly the heart is?'

Patil was quiet for a moment. 'You have a point, sir, but I'm sure the victim would have struggled, and that's when he shifted and got stabbed in the lungs instead.'

'That's the thing, Harish. I don't see any sign of struggle mentioned in the report. Nothing under the victim's fingernails or on his hands, no bruises anywhere on the body. It seems like he was caught completely by surprise and died quickly. You remember the crime scene? There was nothing broken, nothing out of place.'

'I have a theory, sir.' Patil's eyes lit up. 'I think the two of them may have been lying down on that carpet and... er... romancing. She must have been on top and stabbed him when he was totally defenceless. That would explain the lack of bruises or struggle.'

'But Harish, then it would have to be premeditated. If they were having sex on the carpet when it happened, it's hardly likely that Ms Sequeira got up in the middle of it, went to the kitchen and returned with the knife; while Dev lay there quietly. If your theory is correct, she must have kept the weapon close at hand much earlier. And by the way, there's no evidence of sexual intercourse mentioned in the post-mortem.'

Patil sighed. 'Only Ms Sequeira can tell us what really happened that night, sir.'

'There's another thing.' Kabir narrowed his eyes. 'You remember we saw the half-full glasses at Dev's apartment? It was natural for them to have been drinking, as two lovers might on a romantic evening. And the man had a very well-stocked bar.'

'Yes, I remember, sir.'

'And yet, the post-mortem report mentions no trace of alcohol in Dev's blood. Isn't that strange?'

Kabir stood up and added, 'Let's find out how the forensics team is getting along. We need more information, and quickly.'

Forensic science has become crucial in the investigation and detection of crime for the Mumbai Police, with the number of cases being referred to the FSL doubling in the past five years. The FSL in Mumbai was established in 1958 with a handful of experts and has now become a full-size directorate headquartered in Kalina. It also has seven regional units across the state, employing over a thousand people.

The FSL's areas of expertise include toxicology, serology, DNA analysis, ballistics, cyber-forensics and voice authentication. Their work with the Mumbai Police covers a broad spectrum, from identifying dead bodies to providing leads to the culprit and finding court-admissible evidence. However, with the huge caseload at the FSL, reports on routine cases remain pending for several months, even as major crimes like terror acts or gang rape get priority.

The government had recently invested in a number of mobile forensic vans for the city and state police. These vans were equipped with sophisticated equipment to collect blood, fingerprints and other evidence in a scientific manner, and carry out seventeen types of tests at the crime scene itself. The FSL trained many police personnel in basic forensic science and techniques so that they could operate these mobile units and collect the evidence before it got contaminated or destroyed.

After receiving the commissioner's call the previous morning, Patil had spoken to his counterpart at the Bandra thana and commandeered their mobile forensic van. An expert from the FSL had also joined the team at the crime scene, again requested by Patil, but eventually facilitated by the high-level attention the case was getting.

One of the interrogation cells at the Crime Branch headquarters had been converted into a war room for the Dev Malik investigation. When Kabir and Patil walked over, only Nusrat Bharucha, the scientist from the FSL, was sitting there, looking intently at her laptop screen. Young and attractive, Nusrat was a rising star in forensic circles and had worked on several high-profile crimes. The commissioner had personally asked for her to be assigned to the case.

Kabir asked, 'What do we have, Nusrat?'

Nusrat looked up and smiled at him. She had worked with Kabir in the past and been impressed by his powers of deduction as well as his strong but calm personality. In fact, she had to admit to herself that she had developed a bit of a crush on him.

'You've seen the post-mortem report, sir?'

'Yes, and it raises more questions than answers.'

'Exactly. Did you note the lack of alcohol traces in the victim's blood?'

'I did indeed.' Kabir sat on the empty chair next to Nusrat. He could smell her perfume, a complex fusion of floral notes, clearly expensive. 'Any leads from the data on Dev's phone?'

'It appears that he deleted his entire chat history the evening he died, but we still managed to retrieve around a week's worth of data, since the app stores that on the phone itself.'

Patil, who had remained standing behind them, cut in. 'Or maybe the killer deleted it? It seems too much of a coincidence.'

Nusrat turned around and said, 'That can't be ruled out. In fact, the chat with Sharon Sequeira is interesting. They were definitely very lovey-dovey, and it's clear that Dev had invited her over for dinner. He mentions that he had a special evening planned.'

Patil exclaimed, 'And the bitch ended up murdering him!'

Kabir said, 'Mrs Sequeira mentioned to us that her daughter was not her usual self after returning from her clinic, and left home at six. Then, something must have happened in those intervening hours. She must have gone somewhere before landing up at Dev's place. We need to find out where she went.'

'We have a motive now, sir,' interjected Nusrat. 'Perhaps Sharon wanted to delete any incriminating messages and tried to make it look like it was Dev purging the data on his phone. She wouldn't have known that the only foolproof way was to have deleted the app itself.'

'Yes, it certainly looks like that,' said Kabir. 'Was there any evidence on the victim's body?'

'Nothing much. There was hardly any blood spatter, except the pool on the carpet. I've sent his clothes for analysis, but that will take time. If we're really lucky, we'll find some DNA other than his own, but I wouldn't hold my breath on it. I did see some strands of red cotton clearly visible on his black tee, presumably from the woman's dress.'

'And do we have the fingerprint analysis yet, Nusrat?'

'Yes sir, and that's what is a little puzzling.'

'I was just looking at what the lab sent back.' She turned the laptop towards him. There were several purple and grey fingerprint images on the screen, overlaid with arrows and annotations.

Nusrat rolled her eyes. 'It's still mostly manual. Our work would have been so much simpler if only we had access to the Aadhaar database, sir.'

She had raised a sensitive and much-debated topic. As per the Aadhaar Act, the biometrics data collected by the Unique Identification Authority of India or UIDAI can be used only for the purpose of generating Aadhaar, the unique, twelve-digit identity number of over a billion Indians. There have been persistent demands for the police to be given access to the Aadhaar database, for identifying dead bodies, and more importantly, catching first-time criminals. It's a fact that 80 per cent of crimes reported every year are committed by offenders with no police record.

There is a provision in the act permitting limited use of the Aadhaar database in cases involving national security but only after pre-authorisation by a high-powered oversight committee. However, with both the government and the Supreme Court having taken a strong stand regarding data privacy, this exception has never been allowed, despite requests from various states.

Nusrat continued, 'The team managed to lift quite a few prints from the crime scene, but most of them belong to either the victim or his household staff. And yes, we have Sharon Sequeira's prints as well.'

'What about the glasses, Nusrat?'

'The whisky tumbler has Dev's prints, and the wine glass has Sharon's, as expected.' Nusrat paused. 'There was one thing, though. The wine glass looked new, compared to the remaining ones of the set we found in the bar, sir.'

'Are you sure it belongs to the same set?'

'Well, it's the same brand and product. Maybe one had broken recently, and Dev got a replacement. It's an Austrian make, and very expensive.'

'Maybe.' Kabir turned to Patil. 'Harish, ask someone to check where that glass is available in India. If it's so premium, I presume it can't be retailing on Amazon.'

He suddenly looked away, trying to remember something. 'There was no food at the crime scene, right? Nothing served or laid out, I mean. And yet, Dev had prepared quite a spread. Why didn't he bring out the starters with the drinks, I wonder?'

'Yes sir, you're absolutely right. We found that strange too.' Nusrat went on, 'Anyway, Sharon's prints are all over the apartment, which isn't surprising since she was a frequent visitor there. But we found one set on top of the shoe cabinet in the foyer that we haven't been able to identify yet. It's almost a full handprint, and kudos to the constable who noticed the faint smudge, otherwise we'd have missed it.'

'Have you eliminated all our folks and everyone else who was there after the murder last night?'

'Yes, of course.' Nusrat looked pained. 'That's the first thing we did.'

'Sorry, Nusrat. Stupid question. However, what makes you think that it's not an old print?'

'Good question, sir,' said Nusrat a little impertinently. 'The maid told us that she had wiped all the furniture clean that afternoon, including the shoe cabinet, so…'

Kabir interrupted. 'So… there was someone else other than Sharon Sequeira at Dev's apartment that evening.'

10

Tanya stared blankly at Dev's lifeless body, her eyes welling up with tears. The corpse lay on a wooden stretcher and was wrapped in a white sheet. His head had been covered to hide the ugly sutures of the post-mortem, with only the face visible. His final expression was strangely peaceful as if he had already forgiven his killer.

Dev's last rites were being carried out at the Chandanwadi crematorium in Marine Lines, nearly forty-eight hours after his death. The police had finally completed the paperwork and released the body a short while earlier. Vice Admiral Malik, who had made all the arrangements, stood in stoic grief near the splayed feet of his dead son, with Dev's sister next to him.

Tanya glanced at them, caught the hard glare of her sister-in-law, and looked away. She lived with her husband and two children in New York and hadn't been particularly close to Dev. The two women had never liked each other, and things got worse after the estrangement. *Bitch*, thought Tanya.

There was a small, motley group in attendance, all dressed in white. Dev was a popular man, not just with the ladies, and many more people would have liked to have paid their last respects to him. But his father was firm that the cremation be restricted to close family only. In fact, he didn't want Tanya there either but had relented after she called him and insisted.

Tanya knew everyone present, of course. Many of them stole glances at her, and there were brief whispers which she guessed were about her. Since her marriage to Dev, she had always been an object of both fascination and gossip among her in-laws. She had smiled briefly at a couple of the elders earlier, but they ignored her. *It's as if they think that I'm the one responsible for Dev's death.*

After the separation, the Malik family had closed ranks around Dev, and she had been made out to be the villain of the piece. It was assumed and portrayed that she was the one who had strayed. *After all, an actress is supposed to sleep around, isn't she?* Tanya thought bitterly. *If only they knew the truth.* Actually, they knew of Dev's philandering ways only too well but just chose to ignore it.

Unaccountably, an old riddle came to Tanya's mind. A young girl was attending her mother's funeral and saw a strange man there, with whom she fell in love at first sight. After the funeral, she realised that she didn't know his name, and no one else seemed to know who he was either. A few days later, the girl killed her sister. The question was why did she do that? Whoever answered that it was because she hoped to see the man again at her sister's funeral was likely to be a psychopath. *Now why did I think of that?*

When it was Dev's turn to be cremated, a priest performed his last rites. The main hall was closed since a slab had fallen from the ceiling recently, and the lobby where they waited was in crumbling condition too. Ancient ceiling fans hung precariously on rusted rods, with dim tube lights in between. The yellow paint on the walls was faded and peeling. The only furniture was a set of four, moulded-plastic chairs lined up against the wall that opened up into a courtyard. Tanya's eyes went to the hand-painted blackboard declaring that the price for cremating an adult was ₹250, while it was ₹175 for a child. *That's all it costs for a ticket to the other world.*

An hour later, it was over. Dev's ashes were handed over in an urn to his father, and the group slowly trooped out. Tanya waited for the others to leave, and then went up to him. She said softly, 'Papa, you know I loved him dearly. I still do.'

He met her eyes but didn't say anything. Suddenly, Tanya imagined that it was Dev staring at her, and blanched. Her heart tightened. *Is he trying to tell me something from the other side?* She had read that strange things happened when the soul left the body.

She managed to gather herself, touched her father-in-law's feet and stumbled out. There were a few men waiting just outside the gate, and she noticed the cameras in their hands. Bracing herself, she stopped in front of them. Experience had taught Tanya that it was better to do that than try to avoid any interaction altogether. A couple of mikes were pushed in front of her face, while the shutters clicked away.

'Tanya, this side please!'

'Was Dev Malik killed by his new girlfriend?'

'When did you last speak to your husband, madam?'

'Is it true that Jeet has moved in with you?'

There was nothing the paparazzi loved more than capturing an angry reaction on their cameras, and they did everything to provoke their targets. Tanya was well aware of this and forced herself to stay calm. Folding her hands, she said quietly, 'I have no comment. Please leave me alone in this time of grief.'

By this time, Dev's dad had come up behind her. He charged at the journalists, and screamed, 'Get lost, all of you!'

As they retreated, Tanya ran towards her Audi Q3 which the driver had brought up, and jumped in. She looked back through the tinted window and saw her father-in-law shouting and gesticulating furiously even as the men scattered.

She allowed herself a smile.

When Tanya got home, it was Jeet who opened the door, having returned from his recording session earlier than planned.

'How did it go?' he asked.

In response, she hugged him and buried her face in his shoulder. It was a little awkward since he was a few inches shorter than her. She just closed her eyes, for there were no tears left to cry. Jeet patted her head gently, and they stood like that for several moments. He felt no jealousy or resentment. His relationship with Tanya had started as a routine romp and only recently had begun to develop into something more serious. He rationalised that as shocking as it was, Dev's death would force Tanya to finally put him behind her.

She let go of Jeet and flopped down on a beanbag. 'Isn't it strange that you realise how much someone truly means to you only when you lose the person forever?'

Jeet gave a rueful smile. 'Yes, indeed. I know that only too well.' He had lost his wife to cancer a couple of years after moving to Mumbai. It had been an arranged marriage in Guwahati, and she was a pillar of support in all their years together, managing the home and their two sons while he was busy building his musical career. Her death left a sudden and massive void in Jeet's life. He had always taken her for granted until her absence made him realise how much he had actually loved her.

Tanya stared at him, wondering not for the first time why women found him so appealing. Jeet was short and squat, with a large, unremarkable face crowned by a shock of unruly hair. The paunch protruded stubbornly through his loose, silk kurta. His eyes betrayed his Assamese heritage, but the bags under them were entirely the result of too much drinking and an irregular lifestyle. His teeth were permanently stained red by his lifelong addiction to chewing tobacco. No woman would have normally given Jeet a second look.

It's his voice, of course. When Jeet opened his mouth to sing, he transformed into a different person. Even when he performed with just his guitar, it was impossible not to be mesmerised. When a man had talent like that, who cared what he looked like? But unlike his idol, the legendary

Kishore Kumar who had had four wives, all beautiful and talented women who were bowled over by his music, Jeet swore never to marry again.

Tanya asked, 'Have the police contacted you yet?'

'No. Why should they?' He looked startled.

'I forgot to tell you. Yesterday at the apartment, a DCP Kabir Khan and one Inspector Patil had come by and quizzed me about Dev. They want to check my alibi. I guess the spouse is always a prime suspect in any murder.' She rolled her eyes.

'I thought it was his new girlfriend who did it?'

When her father-in-law called late on the night of Dev's murder, Tanya was still awake. Since he never called, and seeing that it was almost dawn, she immediately knew something was wrong. Hearing the news, she screamed and dropped her phone.

Jeet, who was snoring loudly next to her, woke up with a start. He had fallen asleep unusually early that evening, after only his first whisky, and had felt disoriented. He shook his head and said hoarsely, 'What… what was that?'

Tanya's voice was choked. 'It's Dev… he… he's dead.' She buried her face in her hands and began to sob.

Jeet sat up abruptly, and a stabbing pain shot through his head. 'What… How?'

'That bitch… has murdered him.'

11

WHEN Minnie rushed back to India after her mother's sudden and untimely death, a bigger shock awaited her. The suicide note squarely blamed her father for his philandering ways, something that had apparently been going on for many years, and that too with multiple women. Minnie's mother had chosen to turn a blind eye all along, but in the end, she couldn't take it any more.

Minnie's world came crashing down on her. Growing up in what seemed like an idyllic family, she had absolutely no idea of the seething discontent between her parents. Her father would spend long periods away from home, which she always assumed was for his work. Her mother hid her emotions well, never letting Minnie know of the angst raging inside her.

Grief and anger in equal measure threatened to tear Minnie apart. Losing the person dearest to her in such a manner was made even more unbearable by the hatred she began to feel for her father. When he died of a heart attack six months later, Minnie felt no remorse nor did she bother to attend his last rites. She could never forgive him for what he had done to her mother.

After some introspection, Minnie abandoned thoughts of returning to the US to complete her degree at Columbia. She decided to move to Delhi. It was a city she had come to know and love, despite its searing summers and lecherous men.

Minnie knew she had to find a job, and started by contacting the beverage company for whom she had done that landmark commercial. She didn't have any work experience, but she was smart and highly intelligent. Her IQ had been measured at a genius level of 148, and she had joined the elite MENSA society during her brief stint at Columbia. She was confident she could pick up anything very fast.

She didn't have to look any further. The company recognised her potential and made her an offer to join as a graduate trainee, along with a batch they had hired from various campuses. Minnie was thrilled to have landed a job so quickly. She called up her grandmother and promised to send her the first pay cheque, bought herself a new wardrobe of office wear, and threw a party for her college friends at her apartment. She was happy after a long time.

After the initial orientation, Minnie was sent for a month to a bottling plant near Varanasi. The only time she had ever visited a factory earlier was with her father in the tea gardens of Assam. She learnt about the treatment of the water that ensured microbiological safety and the right concentration of salts; the preparation of the syrup with sugar, colour, flavours and concentrate; the final infusion of carbon dioxide to give the characteristic effervescence; and finally, the packaging of the drink into bottles and cans, hermetically sealed, labelled and coded.

However, an even more important learning for her was about the environment and sustainability. Several nearby villages were up in arms against the company, claiming that it was depleting precious groundwater in the arid region, leaving very little for their farms. It wasn't the first time the company had faced such issues, and they had ample resources to handle it. However, the rising unrest had forced them to shelve their expansion plans in the region.

It was Minnie's first visit to Varanasi, and she was fascinated with this most ancient and holiest of cities in the country. She spent hours sitting on the steps of the ghats, watching pilgrims carry out their ritual ablutions, the local priests perform the timeless and spectacular Ganga aarti, and countless bodies being cremated. It made her ponder about the permanence of religion, the futility of life and the inevitability of death. *In the end, it didn't really matter how you lived or when you died.*

Next up was an internship at the company's sales office in Mumbai, which included long visits to the hinterland to understand how the distribution system worked. To Minnie, Mumbai couldn't have been more different from Delhi. The weather, the people, the culture, and the geography of the two metropolises were like chalk and cheese. She didn't much care for the city back then, not knowing yet that it would become her future home. The trips to the interiors on bumpy roads in the sizzling May heat were tough but instructive, and gave Minnie glimpses of the quaint but often harsh realities of rural India.

Then, it was back to the headquarters in Gurugram, where Minnie was asked to work-shadow in different departments for two weeks at a time. She understood how various parts of the corporate machine functioned, and also got valuable insights into office politics, unwritten rules, and gossip-mongering. Six months after she had joined the company, Minnie's induction was over and she had to admit that it had been a terrific experience. She felt ready to take on the world.

Of course, nothing quite so challenging was asked of her, and she was posted as an analyst under one of the brand managers in the marketing department. It was an anti-climax for Minnie after the excitement and variety of the training period, but she jumped into the role with enthusiasm. It entailed a lot of research, analysis of data, and writing of reports. In other words, a blur of slides and worksheets. The hours were long, but her colleagues were nice, and there was a lot of fun and camaraderie at the office.

One day, the marketing director summoned Minnie to his office. Apart from a brief interaction with the top management early on, she had hardly ever seen him. She went for the meeting with trepidation, wondering if something was wrong. The man was a long-timer with the company and touted to be the next CEO. He was sharp and tough, and was known to rip people apart in meetings if they weren't well prepared.

To Minnie's surprise, he was quite charming and immediately put her at ease. He complimented her on her work, to which she responded lamely that she had no idea anyone had noticed, least of all him. He then went on to say that he was going to involve her in a highly confidential project which he was leading, the takeover of a smaller rival. He told her, 'I need a fresh and intelligent mind on this.' She would have to sign a non-disclosure agreement or NDA and work directly with him and a small task force in the due diligence and subsequent negotiations.

Minnie walked out of his office with a smile on her face and a spring in her stride. She knew that companies only deployed their best and brightest in merger and acquisition initiatives, and it was no small matter for a rookie like her to have been selected. What she didn't know was that the much-married man had a habit of preying on young, inexperienced girls by first luring them into his fold, and then using his power and influence to promise them career advancement in return for sexual favours. A corporate casting couch of sorts, as it were, and all too common.

The rest of the team looked askance at Minnie as if they felt she didn't really deserve to be there. Most of them had guessed the real reason anyway. Minnie was determined to earn her place though, and burned the midnight oil to read up on concepts like discounted cash flow or DCF valuation, culture audit, capital structure and post-merger integration. Her job was mainly to prepare presentations based on inputs from others, but at least, she began to understand the content of the slides she was making.

The project ended with a no-go decision by the company's board, but to thank the team for their hard work, the marketing director took them out on a Friday to an exclusive nightclub at a five-star hotel. The drinks flowed freely, and everyone let their hair down. A couple of the men lusted after Minnie, but they were well aware that the boss had his eye on her. And sure enough, he soon pulled her to the dance floor, tottering a little. Minnie enjoyed the attention, and when he offered to drop her home at the end of the evening, she was both relieved and thankful, for it would have been difficult to get a cab at that late hour.

Minnie got into the front seat of the Mercedes, a little surprised that the director himself was driving. As they drove off, he kept looking at her and smiling. It made Minnie uncomfortable, and when he began to compliment her on her dance moves, and her looks and figure, she became downright nervous. It was a long drive, and there was no way she could get off either, at that time of night.

After a spell of silence, the man said that he could help her build a great career with the company, and put his large, hairy hand suggestively on her bare knee. Minnie felt a rush of blood in her head, and swung her fist blindly at him, not knowing her own strength. It landed unerringly on his nose and broke it with an audible crunch. The car swerved and screeched to a stop. Minnie opened the door and without looking back, ran towards an autorickshaw standing a short distance ahead.

The next morning, the HR head of the company called Minnie to his office and asked her to resign immediately. She protested strongly and narrated the sequence of events but to no avail. The organization had decided to protect its executive at all costs. Minnie was threatened that if she decided to fight, she would be eventually fired with a record of serious misconduct, and no company would ever hire her again. She had no option but to comply, thinking bitterly that if this was what corporate life was about, then she definitely had to find some other calling.

An almost psychotic rage engulfed her. *I want to kill that womanising bastard.*

12

'SHE has a thing for you, sir.'

Kabir whirled around. 'Who?'

'Nusrat.' Patil smiled. 'The forensics girl.'

They were sitting in Kabir's office, having lunch. Patil had opened up his tiffin box to find only fruits and a dry salad of moong and chana, much to his dismay. Kabir was wolfing down a large barbeque chicken pizza, which increased Patil's gloom.

'What nonsense!' Kabir waved his hand dismissively. 'You have an overactive imagination, Harish.'

'I know I'm right, sir. It's so obvious just from the way she looks at you.'

Despite his protests, Kabir had sensed it too. Nusrat was undeniably flirtatious when he was around. When she touched his arm to make a point, it was for a tad longer than necessary. When she smiled at him, there was always a hint of suggestion there. And Patil was right. Kabir had felt her staring at him when she thought he wasn't looking.

He was very aware of Nusrat whenever he was around her. He couldn't help noticing the curve of her hips beneath the tight jeans, or the swell of her breasts through the fabric of her shirt. Her perfume was intoxicating, and Kabir couldn't help thinking that she dabbed on a little extra, especially for him. He felt stirrings that he hadn't in a while, but it was accompanied by a wave of guilt. *She's too young, for God's sake, and I'm a married man.*

Kabir had married his college sweetheart, and they had a teenage daughter. His wife was a successful banker. She certainly made way more money than he did on his meagre government salary. That wasn't a problem by itself, for Kabir had a large inheritance. However, over the years, they had drifted apart, as their respective careers kept them busier and busier. The time they spent together was mostly on account of their daughter, at school functions, or lunch at her favourite pizzeria, or a visit to the mall to buy new shoes. It had been ages since the two of them had holidayed anywhere, and sex was a fond but distant memory.

Kabir forced himself to refocus. It was day three of the investigation, and they hadn't made enough headway. The commissioner had called him in the morning, and she was clearly unhappy. Statistics showed that the probability of solving a murder decreased by half after the first forty-eight hours. If you hadn't cracked the case by then, chances were you never would. Sharon Sequeira was still their primary suspect, but she remained elusive.

Kabir had drafted more men into the team, and they had completed the massive task of scanning footage from the nearly five thousand surveillance cameras installed by the Mumbai Police across the city after the 26/11 terror attack. It was a long shot, but they had nothing else to go on anyway. There was no sign of Sharon Sequeira or her car, but after checking out recordings from the various toll booths, they concluded that she hadn't driven out of the city at least.

The questioning of her friend Rhea Menon corroborated the fact that something important had happened in the evening hours before Dev's murder. They needed to find the mysterious woman who had called Sharon, claiming she had proof of Dev's infidelity, and presumably met her after that.

The call was made from a number in the name of a bus driver living in the Dharavi slum. When a constable arrived at his doorstep, he protested ignorance, claiming he had a different phone and number. He was a victim of the identity theft that underpinned the black market of 'ghost' prepaid numbers used by criminals to remain untraceable, the Indian equivalent of burner phones in other countries.

In the meantime, Nusrat had trawled Dev's phone data and social media accounts to obtain an exhaustive list of his friends and acquaintances. She then reached out to each of them through calls, messages and emails, checking if anyone had information that could help the investigation, especially on any enemies Dev might have had. She drew a blank so far, though many responses were pending.

And then Kabir got a break, though it wasn't quite what he was expecting.

A constable knocked and came in. He said hesitantly, 'Sorry to bother you during lunch, sir, but there's a girl here who's insisting on meeting you. She says it's about the Dev Malik case.'

Kabir wiped his mouth with a tissue. 'Send her in.'

The girl was small and mousy and looked to be in her early twenties, but Kabir guessed she was older. Her hair was cut short and parted on one side. She could have passed off as a boy but for the salwar suit and the bright red nails.

'My name is Bhoomi, sir.' Her voice was soft but confident.

Kabir's eyes narrowed. 'What do you want?'

'Thank you for seeing me, sir. I heard about the murder of Dev Malik and decided to come to the police. I've been working as a maid in his building complex, Ocean West, sir.'

Kabir looked at Patil. 'She worked for Dev Malik?'

Bhoomi interjected. 'No, no, sir, not Dev Malik. It was Neena Razdan. She stays with her twin boys and her dog, a German Shepherd, in the same tower as Dev, on the tenth floor. Her husband is something called a partner with some big company. He was offered a transfer to Singapore last year, but she refused to move with him. He went ahead and shifted anyway. It didn't make a big difference because he used to travel a lot even before that.

'I worked for three years at another apartment in Ocean West itself, until the residents decided to move to Bengaluru. Hearing about this opening at Mrs Razdan's place through the staff network, I went over and presented myself for the job. When I first met her, Mrs Razdan seemed quite nice. She quizzed me about my background and experience, and seemed satisfied.' Bhoomi shook her head. 'I had no idea then about what kind of person she really was, sir.'

Patil interrupted. 'What does this Neena Razdan look like?'

'Oh, she's beautiful, sir. Typical Kashmiri looks, fair-complexioned and sharp-featured.'

'What about her figure?'

Kabir shot him a look, and he added, 'I mean... Is she tall or short? Thin or fat?'

Kabir nodded imperceptibly, realising where Patil was going with this line of questioning.

'Oh, she's tall... Much taller than me, sir.' Bhoomi gestured with her hand. 'She's a little plump, I would say. I think it could be because of some medicines she takes for her depression, sir.'

Kabir's interest was piqued. 'Depression?'

'Mrs Razdan used to work for some news channel, sir. Apparently, she had some kind of a nervous breakdown a few years back and quit overnight. There were rumours that she was having an affair with her boss and had been asked to go. Since then, she never took up any other job or maybe couldn't find one.'

'How do you know all this?'

Bhoomi smiled briefly. 'From the driver, sir. The medicines, of course, I saw while cleaning her room.'

'Go on.'

'As I spent more time at the house, I came to the conclusion that Mrs Razdan wasn't mentally stable, sir. She would fly into a rage for no apparent reason, and throw things around. Her two boys bore the brunt of her anger, and she would often hit them. Even that great big dog, which I was petrified of, seemed to be scared of her. Her husband visited one weekend, and she fought continuously with him while he was there. I don't blame the man for running away to Singapore, sir.'

'Doesn't she go out anywhere?'

'She goes once a week to some NGO that works with disabled children. Apart from that, hardly at all.'

Patil asked, 'And how did this Mrs Razdan treat you, Bhoomi?'

'Oh, she was awful, sir.' Bhoomi's eyes flashed with anger. 'She was never happy with anything I did and shouted at me all the time. I have worked in households with unpleasant people but nothing like this woman, sir. It was really hell.

'I had anyway made up my mind to quit, but the last straw came quicker than I had expected, sir. One day, I was cooking breakfast when Mrs Razdan stormed into the kitchen, screaming that her diamond ring was missing and that I had stolen it! Forcing myself to stay calm, I said I would go look for it, knowing that she was absent-minded and often left things all over the place. Sure enough, I found the ring next to the wash basin and handed it to her.'

Bhoomi paused.

'What happened after that?'

'Mrs Razdan... just *slapped* me! It was shocking, to say the least. Something like this has never happened to me, sir. She then continued her accusation, saying that I had returned the ring only because she had caught me out. Can you imagine her nerve, sir? I walked out of the house that very minute, and never went back.'

Kabir made a mental note to check if Neena Razdan had filed a complaint against this girl. It was certainly brave of Bhoomi to come to the police, knowing she could be facing a possible case herself. Her outrage over Neena's behaviour clearly overcame any fear. 'So what's the connection between this woman and Dev Malik?'

'Well, sir, I discovered that they had had an affair in the past. I don't know how exactly it began, but while it was on, they would meet in one of the apartments whenever the respective spouses were away, which was often.

'However, it didn't last long and apparently ended as suddenly as it had started. The gossip goes that Dev called it off, realising too late that this was a dangerous and crazy woman. She took it very badly, and it was a terrible time for everyone in the household.'

'Her husband didn't find out?'

'I think he knew but probably cared less. He's sleeping with a colleague himself, but that's another story.'

'So why are you here, Bhoomi?' Kabir leaned forward. 'Do you think Neena Razdan could have killed Dev Malik?'

'Yes, sir. That's why I'm taking the risk to come to you. That horrible woman deserves to be punished!' She paused. 'A week before his murder, and it was my second last day there, I overheard Mrs Razdan telling someone on the phone, "*My plan is ready. Who knows Dev's routine better than me... That man is as good as dead.*"'

13

NEENA Razdan sat on her balcony, sipping on a steaming cup of kahwa. She had never been to her scenic home state of Kashmir, but her mother had weaned her on the taste of this exotic beverage made up of native green tea, spices, nuts and saffron, and it had remained a lifelong addiction. As she watched the sun begin its journey towards the horizon, she wondered how her life had become such a sorry mess.

Neena came from an accomplished Kashmiri Pandit family, who had left the Valley decades before the mass exodus of the 1990s that accompanied the eruption of militancy in the region. Her father was a noted diplomat, who had served as the country's ambassador to several important countries. Her mother was a proficient artist, who had let different influences hone her skills as she travelled the world with her husband, and exhibited her work whenever they were in Delhi. Neena was not quite as smart or talented and had grown up with an inferiority complex, especially with a sibling who seemed to excel at everything he tried his hand at. Her elder brother would go on to become a professor of physics at Harvard.

After studying in different schools in the various world capitals her father was posted to, Neena eventually pursued a diploma in radio and TV journalism from the Indian Institute of Mass Communication in Delhi. Media, especially television, was growing rapidly in scale and importance, and Neena figured that it was the perfect career for her. She was good-looking enough to be on screen but was too self-conscious, and preferred being on the other side of the camera.

A newly established channel, one of the first to exclusively focus on business news, brought her on board as a production assistant, and it was the start of a decade-long association. Neena loved her job, and worked impossibly long hours along with everyone else, building up the channel's pre-eminence, even as many competitors sprouted. She had remained single, though there was no lack of suitors.

And then, Karan Mehra entered her life. He was a brash but rising star in the industry and was poached by her channel's promoters from a rival. He came in as managing editor, which basically meant that he was the CEO. Karan had strong opinions on everyone and everything and made major changes in the organization, including the sacking of several long-timers. He was a terrific news anchor, with his intense eyes, salt-and-pepper beard and rich baritone, and he overshadowed all the others. He became highly unpopular among his colleagues, but the channel's ratings soared.

Karan realised that Neena was critical to the channel's operations, for she had been there since its inception, and no one could manage all the content, people, creatives and technicals seamlessly as she did. He promoted her to executive producer, making her his de facto deputy. After a few weeks of working closely with Karan, Neena realised that beneath his high-handed, egotistical exterior was a brilliant mind and a surprisingly affectionate heart. She fell hopelessly in love with him.

Karan was married and generally a faithful husband, but he wasn't immune to Neena's considerable charm and attention. At a company off-site in Goa, they ended up sleeping together. For Neena, it was the most blissful night of her life, but for Karan, it sparked off a storm of guilt and remorse. When they returned to Mumbai, he called Neena to his office and told her that it had been a big, alcohol-induced mistake. He asked her to forget about the whole thing.

Neena was furious and promised herself that it wasn't going to be the end of it. For the next few days, she pretended to be perfectly normal with him, focusing on their work together, as if nothing had happened. Karan was relieved, but he had completely missed the infatuated look in her eyes whenever they met. The truth was that her obsession with him was increasing with each passing day.

It started with the late-night messages, telling him how she felt about him and reminding him of Goa. After a while, Karan stopped responding so she began calling him at home at odd hours. The work emergency excuse only went so far, and his wife got suspicious. Each morning, Karan found a rose on his desk, and everyone in the office knew who was putting them there. One day, Neena cornered him in his cabin and begged him to sleep with her just one more time, promising that she would not bother him after that. Karan finally lost his cool and screamed at her. As Neena stormed out, she realised that her colleagues who were sitting just outside had heard everything.

That evening, she ordered two strips of sleeping pills from her local chemist and consumed them.

The doorbell rang, and Neena got up to open the door. It was Kabir.

'Good evening, Mrs Razdan. I'm DCP Kabir Khan from the Crime Branch. I'd like to have a word with you.'

'What's this about?' Neena asked frowning, though she knew only too well. She stood in a statuesque pose, one arm akimbo and the other raised against the door frame. Bhoomi has described her well, Kabir thought. She had been beautiful once, though her face was now puffy and there were dark bags under her eyes. Her voluptuous figure was wrapped in a black silk nightgown.

'Can we talk inside?' Kabir replied firmly. 'It's about the murder of Dev Malik.'

She led him to the balcony and offered him kahwa, but he declined politely. They sat down on the faux cane chairs.

'It's a beautiful view, isn't it?' Neena stared out at the sea, a faraway look in her eyes. She crossed her legs, and her gown fell away, revealing an expanse of thigh.

'Uh… Yes indeed.' Kabir cleared his throat. 'How well did you know Dev Malik?'

'Know who?' She seemed distracted. 'Ah yes, Dev.'

'Yes?'

'Dear Dev. Such a good-looking man.' She shook her head. 'And nice too, which is rare.'

'So you knew him well?'

'Knew him well?' She gave a husky laugh. 'I had sex with him. So yes, you could say I knew him well.'

Kabir wasn't expecting such a direct answer, but he pressed on. 'And when was this?'

'When?' Neena giggled. 'At all times of the day, DCP Kabir, but I preferred the afternoons.'

'You know what I mean, ma'am,' said Kabir sternly. 'Please answer the question.'

She pouted. 'Let me see… I first met Dev last year. It was 31st December, I remember.'

She had been dragged to the New Year's Eve bash at Otter's Club by an old girlfriend who was visiting her from London. Neena didn't like loud music or partying, but her friend had just had a nasty break-up with her Scottish partner and needed cheering up. Besides, her own husband was in New York, wrapping up a project with a global insurance client, and she figured that spending the evening out wouldn't be such a bad thing.

To her surprise, Neena enjoyed herself thoroughly. The live band kept going off-key and played Bollywood songs Neena had never heard before, but it didn't matter. The heaving crowd jived and swayed to the catchy beats, and the mood was infectious. The two of them drank and danced the night away. At the stroke of midnight, Neena found herself wishing and hugging several random people, but it all seemed perfectly normal.

When they finally came out at one-thirty in the morning, Neena discovered that her driver's phone was switched off. They walked up and down the lane adjacent to Joggers Park where all the cars were parked, but couldn't locate her black SUV, so they went back to the club gate. A man was standing there, reading messages on his mobile, and looked up at them.

It was Dev. He smiled and said, 'Happy New Year, ladies.'

Neena hadn't seen a more attractive man in a long time. She stared at him, unable to speak.

'Happy New Year to you, sir,' her friend said. 'Were you there inside? I'm sure I'd have remembered.' She giggled drunkenly.

'No, I wasn't. I came to pick up someone, but it looks like she's left already.'

A sleek Jaguar pulled up in front. Dev started to walk towards it, then stopped and turned back. 'Can I drop you somewhere?'

Neena found her voice. 'Yes, would you please? My driver seems to have disappeared.'

As they got into the car, she said, 'We need to get to Worli. I hope it's not too far out of your way.'

'I'm heading there myself. Ocean West.'

Neena exclaimed, 'Oh, that's where I live!'

Dev looked back from the front passenger seat. 'Now isn't that some coincidence…'

'We moved in a couple of months ago.'

The two of them chatted animatedly after discovering they were neighbours. Neena's friend was quiet but kept nudging her and giggling audibly.

The drive got over all too quickly. As Neena thanked Dev and gave him a lingering hug, she couldn't help admitting to herself that he had already made a devastating impression on her. *I haven't felt this way since... Karan.*

'It turned out Dev already knew my husband professionally, having worked together on a project for a start-up he had invested in. So I invited him and his wife over for dinner one evening. Tanya's an actress, as you know. She's really snooty and had this patronising air which I found intolerable. The evening turned out to be incredibly boring, except for Dev, of course. The four of us met once or twice after that, but it was clear we weren't going to become great friends.

'Dev and I bumped into each other at the local supermarket one day, and we decided to go for a coffee from there. That's when we realised that we had so much more to talk and laugh about than when our spouses were around. Initially, I didn't let on about how I felt about him. But one thing led to another. We were two people in lonely marriages and getting into a relationship seemed almost natural.'

Kabir asked, 'Did your husband know?'

Neena made a face. 'He's only focused on his work. It's all that matters to him. I think he knew but didn't care. You see, the two of us, my husband and I, were set up by a common friend and rushed into marriage too quickly. It's my first and his second. We realised too late that it was a big mistake, and now we're stuck with each other. In a way though, it's actually convenient because he does care for me at some level, and I don't mind living like this.' She waved her hands around.

'For how long did your affair with Dev go on?'

Neena put her hand on Kabir's arm and looked him deep in the eyes. 'DCP Kabir, do you know what it's like to love someone more than your own life?'

'I...'

'You're a strong man, I can feel it.' She leaned over and closed her eyes. 'You smell nice. Very masculine.'

Kabir gently removed her hand and sat up straight. 'Mrs. Razdan, you really must...'

She interrupted. 'I can see from the ring that you're married. How much do you really love your wife?'

Kabir raised his voice. 'Please, ma'am. I'm the one asking the questions here.'

She got up abruptly and went inside. Kabir wondered whether to follow her, but she returned quickly. There was a pack of Benson & Hedges in her hand. 'Do you mind, officer?'

'Go ahead.'

She opened the pack and held it out to him, but he declined, albeit reluctantly. Though not a regular smoker, he didn't mind an odd cigarette, especially if someone offered one. However, he didn't want Neena to think that this was anything but a serious interrogation.

She lit a cigarette and took a long pull. 'The last time I felt this way about a man, I almost died. Thankfully, all I ended up losing was my job. With Dev, it was different. I thought he loved me too. There was so much passion between us, and I don't mean just in the bedroom.'

Neena stopped speaking and hung her head. Kabir thought she was crying, but she suddenly looked up, and her eyes were blazing. 'That bastard! He couldn't keep it in his pants. That was his bloody problem.'

Kabir was taken aback.

She continued, her voice rising. 'I caught Dev cheating on me, the two-timing scoundrel! People had warned me about his womanising, but I was the idiot who didn't listen. When I found him with that dentist in his apartment, I felt like killing both of them!'

Kabir said softly, 'And now, he's dead.'

Neena whirled around towards him. 'You think I murdered Dev?'

He held her gaze but didn't say anything.

'You do, don't you?' She stubbed out the cigarette. 'That's why you're here.'

'We're exploring all angles.' After a pause, he asked, 'Where were you the night Dev was murdered?'

Neena was silent for a moment. Then she said defiantly, 'I was at home. Alone.' She abruptly caught both his hands in hers. 'If you think I killed Dev Malik, you can arrest me right now, DCP Kabir!'

Kabir freed himself from her surprisingly strong grip, and glared at her.

'Sorry, I… don't know what I was thinking.' She sounded deflated. 'You know, Dev and I hadn't spoken since… the break-up, but I could never really get over him. Sometimes, I would see him in the complex, looking as handsome and dashing as ever, and my heart would ache. I knew his marriage was over, and he was living alone. That other woman was still in his life. But I always thought she wasn't his type and it would end sooner or later.

'But… it didn't end. That bitch had some strange hold over Dev. Someone told me he was serious about her, but I couldn't believe it. Dev Malik and serious about a woman? No way! One part of me had hoped that since Tanya was out of the picture, I could maybe try to get back into Dev's life. I never stopped loving him, you know. In fact, I became even more obsessed with him after we broke up. But it wasn't to be…'

Kabir wondered why she was opening up to him like this. She was being either very naive or very devious, he couldn't tell.

The woman was unstable, that was for sure. And undoubtedly dangerous.

14

THE cashier looked up and asked, 'Sharon Sequeira?'

'Yes, that's my credit card.'

'Do you have any other cards?'

She shook her head. 'Why, isn't this one working?'

He stood up. 'Please wait. I'll just be back.'

'Is there a problem?'

'No problem, ma'am.' There was uncertainty in his voice. 'It'll only take a minute.'

She saw him walk towards a man standing in the central aisle. He was wearing a tie, clearly some sort of a supervisor. They had a brief conversation, glanced at her and then headed for a door marked 'For Authorised Personnel Only'.

She immediately realised that something was wrong. *The credit card must have been hotlisted by the police.* Luckily for her, it was a tap-and-pay transaction and the card was still in her hand. The bill had already been printed and was lying next to the register. She casually picked up the paper bag containing her purchases, grabbed the bill, and made for the exit. The guard there looked perfunctorily inside her bag, punched the bill and waved her on.

Her car was some distance away, on a parallel road, for there wasn't any parking near the store. In hindsight, she was thankful because if indeed the police had been alerted, as was very likely, they were bound to check all the CCTV cameras in the immediate vicinity of the store. She had ditched the Honda Jazz and got a rental, but she didn't want them to know its licence plate number. While walking towards it, she deftly changed her appearance by covering her head with a colourful bandana.

As she drove out of the city, she thought about the past few days. It had been tumultuous, to say the least. The chain of events set off by Dev's death was still playing out. When she was growing up, her mother would often say to her that if you tell a lie, you'll need to tell many more lies to cover it up. In a way, that was what was happening with her now. Except that it wasn't just a lie she was covering up. And unexpected things had happened, as they tend to do.

Why the hell did Dev have to be the way he was? It was really all his fault. She didn't feel any guilt, any remorse. He had got what was coming to him. *Cheating bastard. It was incredible how he could be so charming and deceitful at the same time.* She had met her share of scoundrels in the past but none quite like Dev. *Someone should make a movie about his life. And his death.*

She crossed the newly constructed Panvel toll naka, which wasn't yet operational, and was soon on the Expressway. It was always a pleasure to drive on what used to be the best road in the country until a few years ago. Unlike the blacktop highways in the north and south, this one was built of concrete, because of the heavy rains in the monsoons. That was also the season when the drive was the most beautiful, with a brooding grey sky above and lush greenery on either side. The clouds always threatened to burst and often did, creating a blinding wall of water that seemed almost impossible to break through.

There was no such weather that day, for it was January and the sky was a clear blue. The ghat section began and a short while later, she turned off into a narrow road. It wound its way through dense woods for five kilometres, traversing the length of a ridge before ending at an imposing signboard with the name of a prominent city builder.

It was a vacation home development situated on a small plateau, surrounded by the Khandala hills. Most of the individual plots were fenced off and had houses in various stages of construction. There had been some trouble with local permissions which needed an unusual amount of time and bribes that had to get fixed.

She drove towards a quaint yellow villa, one of the few which was already completed. It was situated at one edge of the property, overlooking a steep cliff. The place was perfect for her purposes, totally remote and secluded. She opened the automated sliding gate with a remote control and parked the car in the covered porch. There was a spectacular panoramic view from the spot, but it didn't interest her. Unlocking the front door, she quickly went inside.

There was a spacious drawing-cum-dining room, not yet fully furnished, leading into two bedrooms and a smaller study. She threw her handbag and the groceries on top of an antique wooden cabinet in the foyer and sank into the plump leather sofa.

This really can't go on for much longer. I need to end it soon. One way or another.

She took a deep breath. An unforeseen circumstance had delayed everything. It was part bad luck, and part error in judgement. Nevertheless, she knew how to handle it. It would take another twenty-four hours, maybe less. She had come this far and wouldn't let anything or anyone stop her.

There was a scratching sound from one of the bedrooms. She sighed and got up.

The old man saw her drive in, from his gazebo across the road. That plot belonged to his son, who had bought it many years ago when the builder launched the project with much fanfare. But he moved to Paris soon after that and had to abandon his plans of building a vacation home there. Because of the environmental issues, everything was stalled for a long time anyway.

The old man was a widower, leading a quiet retired life at his tiny apartment in Chembur. His son wanted to move him to a larger and more comfortable place, but he had refused, not wanting to leave the home he had lived in for three decades. However, after reading in the newspapers that the Khandala property was finally cleared for construction, he drove up there the next day.

With the help of a local architect, he designed an outhouse studio, big enough for one person to stay in. It was shaped like a gazebo with tall, mullioned windows and a gabled roof. It was built on the highest point of the land, leaving ample space for the main house, as and when that would be constructed. The man used up his own savings, reasoning that he was doing this only for himself. His son pleaded that he be allowed to fund the project but to no avail.

The man loved his little hill getaway and would spend weeks at a time there. He had set up a small vegetable garden, while everything else was available at the hamlet nearby. During the day, he would go for long walks or sit on the patio, reading a book. Nestled in the lap of nature, he had even rediscovered his college pastime of writing poetry. When night fell, he stayed indoors with a glass of whisky, since there were a pair of leopards known to be in the area, seen often on CCTV cameras.

He knew of his neighbour and had often thought of going over to introduce himself but had never summoned up the courage. She rarely visited anyway, that too never on her own. Not that it was appropriate for him to be seeking company from a woman less than half his age. He blushed at the very thought. He was lonely and was waiting eagerly for the day when more of the houses would be completed and people would start moving in.

However, over the past few days, there had been plenty of activity in the yellow villa. The man remembered being woken up late one night by the grating sound of a car braking suddenly on gravel. He was surprised, for no one ever came in or out of the property at that hour. He himself had just arrived earlier that day, after a spell of over two months in the city. The power had gone so he took a torch in his hand before stepping out onto his patio.

It was dark, but he saw a white car parked in front of the villa. Since it hadn't been there earlier in the evening, he presumed it was the one that had just driven in. There was still a faint swirl of dust and smoke lingering behind it. He knew that she had a dark-coloured SUV, so this was definitely a different vehicle.

All the curtains were drawn, but he could make out someone moving inside the house with possibly a mobile phone torch. There was suddenly a muffled scream and a thud, followed by the light going off. Then, there was silence even as the man strained to see or hear more. Sound travelled clearly, especially through the open spaces and clean air. He worried that she might have hurt herself and was debating whether to go over to check when the light came back on. There was a new, scraping noise of something heavy being dragged on the floor.

It was cold, and the man shivered. He had rushed out without his shawl. A new sound came to his ears, much closer this time, like the rustle of an animal moving through a bush. He realised that it was from his own compound. Knowing that it was most likely a rabbit or mongoose but not wanting to take any chances, he went back inside reluctantly and closed the door. He lay awake for some time, but all was quiet. When he went outside first thing the next morning, the car was gone.

Since then, the car would be back almost daily but always after sunset. He only caught brief glimpses of her, for she stayed inside all the time. That was unusual because, in the past, he had seen her spend a lot of time in the garden, which was nicely landscaped and had a paved sit-out area sheltered by a white canopy.

In fact, he wasn't even 100 per cent sure that it *was* her. Her head was always covered by a cap or a scarf. That would make sense in the city but certainly not in this remote place. He realised that he hadn't seen her face clearly during these past few days. It seemed like she was deliberately trying to avoid being recognised. Again, that hadn't been the case during her past visits. In fact, she had even smiled at him once when he walked by her gate.

He wondered if something had happened to her, or if this other woman, if it really was someone else, had somehow got possession of the property. But he had checked and was pretty sure that couldn't be true. It was, of course, entirely possible that the recent visitor was a friend or relative of hers, and had her permission to use the place. *Still, something doesn't seem right.*

The funny thing was that even when the car wasn't there, he could have sworn that there was someone still inside the villa.

In today's age, the police track the digital footprints of fugitives primarily through their usage of mobile phones and the internet, both so pervasive that it becomes impossible for anyone, even a person running from the law, to avoid them. Gone are the days of surveillance stakeouts, car chases and meetings with informants in bars.

Call detail records or CDR are now a routine part of any investigation, and telecom providers have to mandatorily share the list of calls made by suspects with the police. Tech-savvy criminals use internet-based telephony, which makes detection more difficult. In this case, terabytes of internet Protocol Detail Records or IPDR—apps used, websites visited, IP addresses to which messages have been sent—have to be painstakingly analysed.

Location tracking of mobiles is another common tool for the police. Again, seasoned offenders are able to switch phones or use them only for short durations to avoid getting caught. However, they often forget to be as careful about their social media activities and get tripped up by a selfie or status update posted on Facebook or Twitter. For example, a Delhi gangster uploaded a video of his birthday bash, which gave the police clues to his hideout, resulting in his arrest.

Not only are cybercrime units 'monitoring and patrolling' social media nowadays, but they are also leveraging popular platforms to reach out to citizens to help them find a missing person or catch various categories of offenders like kidnappers, pickpockets, chain-snatchers and eve-teasers. Besides, thousands of traffic violators are caught by photos or videos submitted on the Facebook pages of city police forces.

All these tools had been activated in the hunt for Sharon Sequeira. The CDR had only led to dead ends, and the Crime Branch waited for her to switch on her mobile, but she never did. They figured that maybe she had got herself another connection which couldn't be traced back to her. There were no social media updates. In fact, she didn't even have a Facebook or Instagram account.

Sharon's credit and debit cards had been hotlisted by the police, but the problem was that there was no way for the acquirer networks to flag the reason for it or assign any specific priority. If someone tries to use a hotlisted card at any point-of-sale terminal, the transaction gets reported to the issuing bank which then analyses the information and passes it along to their own fraud management department or to external agencies, as appropriate.

When the attempted transaction by her credit card at the supermarket in Vashi was reported to the bank's Chennai back office, it somehow got tagged to a lost card report which then went to the suspicious transaction monitoring team in the same unit for further action. Because the system showed that the card hadn't been declared lost by the user, the transaction was parked as an inconsistency to be investigated later, instead of being reported immediately to the Cyber Cell of the Crime Branch.

15

Tanya couldn't shake the feeling that someone was following her.

She rarely drove herself, but it had been a necessity that day. She was on the Eastern Express Highway and looked again in the rear-view mirror. Sure enough, the white sedan was fifty feet behind, as it had been for the past several kilometres.

Normally, she wouldn't have thought much of it, for the vehicle could have been any of the app cabs or rental cars that dotted the city's roads. But it had stopped at the same highway petrol pump where she had tanked up, without anyone getting out or taking any fuel, and then started after her as soon as she drove off. Tanya had first noticed it then, for it was the only other car at the pump, and filed away the licence plate number in her mind. Years of being in showbiz had honed her senses to be on automatic alert for any possible threat.

She wasn't unduly worried though, for she was confident of handling herself in such situations. There was a can of Mace in her handbag at all times. In any case, this was really nothing compared to the incident a couple of years back, when a persistent stalker had made her life hell for a few months.

It had begun with a series of luxurious gifts delivered anonymously at her apartment building. There was a designer bag, an uber-expensive perfume, high-heeled shoes and a red cocktail dress. Usually, her fans would leave letters, or a photo, or flowers at the most. The decent ones, that is. This one seemed to be more sophisticated and clearly rich. To Tanya's surprise, she found each item to be quite to her own tastes and the dress was just the right size. She was tempted to keep them, but something told her not to.

A handwritten note followed, asking Tanya to put on the ensemble of the earlier gifts and go out for dinner with the sender. It was just signed 'A'. She wondered if it might be a genuine suitor after all. There was never any dearth of admirers in her life, from co-actors to corporate honchos and even old acquaintances who would periodically surface to bask in her fame. But none of them was likely to woo her in this cryptic manner.

Tanya decided to report the matter to the police. They took the complaint seriously, especially since the media loved to follow celebrity stalking. However, the man had covered his tracks quite well. The gifts had been bought from different stores, and paid for by cash. One salesgirl remembered the customer, and described him as being young and casually dressed, almost like a college-goer. But she couldn't recall enough of his face for the sketch artist to work on.

The courier company that had done the deliveries wasn't of much help either, for the sender details in each case turned out to be fake. The handwriting on the note was analysed by an expert, who corroborated that the writer was young, and added that he was probably shy, self-critical and impatient, but also very ambitious. There was nothing to do but wait for his next move. Tanya turned down the police's offer of posting a constable at her building, asserting that she didn't feel threatened yet.

It was October, and Tanya was invited to be the chief guest at a prominent Durga Puja pandal in the suburbs. She had no hesitation in accepting, for it was a festival close to her heart. After the inauguration, she spent some time chatting with the organisers, sampling street-food delicacies from the various stalls and generally soaking in the atmosphere. It all reminded her of the revelry during her childhood.

While Tanya was the cynosure of all eyes, there was one youth who caught her attention. He was in his late twenties, his long hair pulled back with a band, and dressed in a T-shirt and faded jeans. Tanya noticed that his sneakers were an incongruously expensive designer brand. He always seemed to be at the forefront of the crowd that followed her around, and there was a strange, fixed expression on his face.

Tanya suddenly remembered the police profile of the man who had been sending her gifts and wondered if this might be him. On an impulse, she turned towards him and asked for his name. His eyes went wide, even as the rest of the people looked at him with interest. He walked away abruptly without responding. Tanya was about to go after him but realised it wouldn't have been appropriate for the occasion.

She asked one of the organisers if she knew who he was, but she shook her head stating that he definitely wasn't one of the regulars, nor did he seem to be from the neighbourhood. Tanya figured her suspicion was proved correct by the man's reaction and even though she didn't know his name, she would now be able to recognise him at least.

For the next few weeks, there were no more gifts or letters. Tanya took this as further evidence that it was indeed the youth from the pandal. Maybe he had been scared off, thinking she was on to him. Then one day, she found an envelope in her mailbox containing a rambling but elaborate marriage proposal. There was no signature, but the handwriting was unmistakable. Besides, there was a veiled reference to their meeting at the Durga Puja inauguration. It had been sent by regular post and was impossible to trace.

There was no further doubt that the young man was stalking her. He seemed to be far more determined and resourceful than anyone earlier. Based on her description of him, the police artist created a reasonable identikit. For the first time ever, Tanya decided to get herself a bodyguard, who went everywhere with her. But she still refused any protection at her home.

More gifts, including a platinum ring that fitted her perfectly and love letters sent by snail mail, followed. The youth was careful not to contact her over any digital media at all. Even if he was tracking her fan pages and social accounts, he remained invisible. Though he hadn't been an overt threat yet, Tanya remained in a constant state of unease. She knew stalkers were unstable, and could do something dramatic at any time.

It happened soon enough. Late one evening, the doorbell rang at Tanya's apartment and she opened the door, assuming it was the pizza she had ordered. Instead, it was the young man from the pandal. He was even dressed exactly the same as then. She screamed and tried to close the door, but he pushed his way inside and said softly, 'Don't be scared. I wouldn't dream of hurting you.'

Her heart beating furiously, Tanya shouted, 'Get out of here! Otherwise, I'll call the police.'

'Can I please say…'

Just then, the doorbell rang again. In a flash, Tanya shoved the youth away and opened the door.

It was the pizza delivery boy this time. His bright, rehearsed smile froze on his lips when he saw the look on Tanya's face. She screamed, 'Help me!'

Together, they managed to restrain the stalker, who seemed resigned and didn't struggle much. It turned out that he was the son of a rich investment banker, and had been obsessed with Tanya for years. When the police took him away, he simply looked back at her and mouthed, 'I'll always love you.'

Tanya smiled ruefully as she remembered the youth. If anything, she had felt mildly sorry for him later. He wouldn't have harmed her in any way, she was sure.

A loud honk from behind broke her reverie and brought her back to the present. The tail was much closer now. She saw that a signal was coming up, where she would be turning off the highway. *Will he try something when I stop?*

She checked that all her doors were locked, and took out the Mace from her bag.

Her pursuer stopped right next to her and rolled down the tinted driver's window. It turned out to be a woman. She was wearing a peaked cap, and Tanya was certain she had seen her somewhere before. She stared malevolently at Tanya, who fumbled for her mobile phone. *Let me take a photo of the bitch, whoever she is.* Just then, the lights changed and the traffic moved ahead. The white sedan continued on straight, even as Tanya took the right turn.

She felt relieved but also intrigued. It was clear that the strange woman had been following her, but why? She wondered if it had anything to do with Dev's death.

Minnie's first meeting with Dev at the cafe in Paris didn't lead to anything right then, despite the obvious attraction between the two. They chatted away until the rain stopped, and then Minnie left. She had promised herself a solo vacation and didn't want any dalliance, however tempting, to change that.

Back in India, she got a call from an unknown number one day. 'Why haven't you called me yet, as promised?'

Minnie instantly knew it was Dev. She replied tartly, 'I was waiting to see if you would.'

He invited her to dinner, and she found herself accepting without hesitation. Dev chose an exclusive, members-only lounge on the top floor of a five-star hotel. It had a sweeping view of the Arabian Sea and was both romantic and private.

'I've never been here,' she said. 'It's beautiful, Dev.'

'We should have done this earlier.'

She just smiled.

Dev wanted to get a bottle of champagne, but she shook her head, opting for a gin and tonic instead. He took the same for himself and insisted on ordering most of the starters on the menu, from the crispy calamari to the edamame dumplings.

Minnie laughed. 'You must think I don't get to eat?'

Dev looked sheepish. 'Actually, it's me who's hungry. I missed lunch today.'

'You poor, starved man.'

'Not so poor, I must admit.'

And so the evening went on. Dev wanted to hear all about Minnie's life and though usually reticent, she found herself telling him everything. *Well, maybe not everything.* Dev had a ready trove of amusing stories to regale women, but for a change, he spoke more about his childhood and his family, how his grandfather had influenced his destiny, and why he felt lonely despite a hectic social life. He couldn't recall when he had last opened up so much to someone he barely knew.

They left only at midnight. Dev dropped her home and stopped himself from asking if he could come up. Somehow, it felt different with Minnie and he didn't want to rush anything. She was mildly disappointed but remembered that she had a flight to catch the next morning.

They would meet again soon enough, though.

16

KABIR took a sip of Jack Daniels and popped a galouti into his mouth.

It was his favourite kebab but not easily available in Mumbai, at least not the authentic one. The galouti is a culinary innovation dating back to the eighteenth century, when a nawab in Lucknow, who was very old and had lost all his teeth, asked his khansama to prepare a kebab that needed no chewing but had the same rich taste and flavour. Thus was born the melt-in-the-mouth delicacy, cooked with tender lamb mince mixed with hundreds of spices and marinated for several hours. After much trial and error, Kabir had found a hole-in-the-wall eatery in Byculla with a chef who hailed from Lucknow and who made the most outstanding galoutis he had ever eaten.

Kabir was sitting in the alcove adjoining the large living room. The French-style windows ran along the entire length of the wall, and he could see the lights of Regal cinema and the evening traffic on the Colaba

Causeway in the distance. It was his favourite spot in the only place he had ever considered home.

When Kabir had hesitantly suggested to his then-fiancée that they should live at his parents' apartment after marriage, she had initially blown her top and threatened to break up the engagement. But she couldn't deny that the location was perfect, not only being one of the most coveted addresses in the city but also close to both their workplaces. There was no way they could have afforded a place anywhere south of Bandra on their own. Besides, it was tempting to move into a fully functional and spacious home, with experienced and tenured household staff, not to mention the best possible babysitters whenever the time came.

In the end, it didn't take much persuasion to change her mind. Kabir heaved a sigh of relief, for he couldn't bear the thought of living anywhere else. He did go away for long periods on his initial postings, but the thought of the familiar and much-loved apartment waiting for him back in Mumbai was never far away.

His wife chose not to move around with him, as she was charting her own career in the financial capital. Kabir didn't mind that, since the living conditions in the interiors were not easy to adjust to, even for him. In the meantime, his parents decided to slow down their legal work and renovated an ancestral villa they owned in Kasauli. Soon, they began to spend a lot of time there, enjoying the clean air and salubrious climate away from the concrete jungle of the metropolis. Kabir's wife didn't mind having the house to herself, though she did miss him terribly at times, at least in the early days of their marriage.

That day, it was Kabir who was alone at home. He wasn't particularly social himself, and the parties they went to were usually invitations from his wife's friends and colleagues. He enjoyed solitude and liked nothing better than making an evening out of whisky and kebabs, and a thriller, be it a book or a movie. But he wasn't able to focus on any fictional plot, since the real-life murder mystery of Dev Malik occupied his mind.

Instead, he had dimmed the lights in the room and switched on his new Echo. The melodious tunes of the sitar played by the peerless Ravi Shankar accompanied by the mesmerising rhythm of the tabla in the hands of the great Alla Rakha filled the room. For decades, these two maestros had spread the gospel of Indian music around the world, their concerts characterised by the complex dialogues between their two instruments. Hindustani classical music never failed to have a soothing effect on Kabir's mind, especially when many thoughts were racing through it.

What had started as an apparently open-and-shut case had already taken many twists and turns. Something had told Kabir early on that this wasn't going to be a straightforward investigation, and he was right. Sharon Sequeira remained missing, though she was by no means the only suspect any more. There were unexplained bits of evidence, inconsistent with the chain of events that the police had pieced together. And new facts were emerging every day.

The meeting with Neena Razdan had been interesting, to say the least, though Kabir couldn't make up his mind about her. She had both the motive and means to have committed the murder. Yet, she seemed too spaced out and even neurotic to have planned and carried out such a crime. *Or maybe that's what she wants people to think.*

Something suddenly struck Kabir. He picked up his phone and dialled SI Patil.

'Hello, sir.' Patil sounded like he had food in his mouth.

'Good evening, Harish. If you're having dinner, I can call back.'

'No, I'm done.' There was a pause, and he added in a whisper, 'Anyway, it was just boiled vegetables and a bowl of daal. I tell you, sir, I'll fall sick from this diet before losing a single kilo.'

Kabir chuckled. 'It's for your own good, Harish. Keep it up, my friend.'

There was only a snort in reply.

'Anyway, I called to ask you something. Did we review the CCTV footage from the lifts in Dev's building?'

Patil thought for a moment. 'Yes, we did, sir. Are you looking for anything in particular?'

'I want to know if Neena Razdan went anywhere in the lift that evening.'

'Okay, I'll get it checked right away, sir.'

'Thank you, Harish.'

'Oh, by the way, I just remembered. There are four lifts, but the CCTV camera was working in only two of them.'

'So we won't know for sure…'

'Apparently, it's been that way for a while, sir. The managing committee of the society has decided to upgrade the entire security system of the building, and they've shortlisted two companies after a bidding process. The chairman is pushing a third one, which he claims is the best in the business, and has accused another committee member of bribery and corruption. There's now a bitter deadlock on the issue, and they won't fix the cameras until a conclusion is reached.'

'And the residents know about this?'

'Yes, sir. It seems that at one committee meeting, two members almost got into a fist fight, and had to be separated by the others. Both are in their sixties. Everyone heard about that incident. Not only that, the residents have now been dragged into the matter, with both factions using the WhatsApp groups to push their respective stands.'

'I see.' Kabir hung up.

So it was possible that Neena Razdan had gone up to Dev Malik's apartment that night, knowing fully well she wouldn't be caught on the CCTV cameras.

The food-delivery platforms offered a bewildering array of choices, but Kabir had already decided on biryani for dinner.

It was one of his favourite dishes though his wife didn't like it at all, only making an exception on Eid in deference to his parents' sensibilities. She was more of a seafood lover and didn't enjoy the meats as much as he did. Nor was she a foodie like him. On the rare occasions when they went out for a meal together, it was tough to decide on a cuisine that both could enjoy.

Kabir had ordered from a Bengali restaurant, which specialised in the Kolkata version of the highly popular dish. The modern biryani developed in the royal kitchens of the Mughal Empire as a fusion of the spicy rice preparations of India and the Persian pilaf, and is today highly popular throughout the subcontinent with many regional variations.

Kabir had visited Kolkata only once, during his deputation with the CBI. It was a murder involving the scion of a prominent Marwari business family. After the initial hush-up, a local newspaper did an exposé and levelled accusations of corruption in the police and political interference in the judicial system. There was a hue and cry, and the CBI was brought in to take over the case.

The investigation went on for two weeks and was inconclusive. Evidence had been destroyed and witnesses compromised. The family was powerful, and their influence ran deep within the establishment. The CBI team wasn't able to implicate the primary accused, but they at least managed to exonerate the young schoolteacher who had been made the scapegoat.

Kabir wasn't impressed with the city. The victim had lived in Shyambazar, and he was forced to tramp through the byzantine lanes of north Kolkata to question various people. It was June, and terribly humid. The only other option was to take a hand-pulled rickshaw, which he refused to do, seeing the plight of the tanned, emaciated rickshaw pullers. Then, the cheap hotel he was put up in had bedbugs and terrible service, neither of which made any concession for the CBI. The case remained a blot in Kabir's book, for he knew that the spoiled, rich kid was indeed the culprit, but they just couldn't prove it.

The only cherished memory from the trip for Kabir was his introduction to the Kolkata biryani.

As he dug into the biryani at his Mumbai apartment that evening, Kabir thought it was damn near as authentic as it could get, even if the accompanying raita was a tad too sweet for his taste. He was thankful that at least his daughter's palate was similar to his, and she absolutely loved all forms of biryani.

Kabir finished his dinner and got up to clear the dishes when his phone rang. He looked at the time, wondering who could be calling at that late hour.

'Hello, Inspector Kabir?' It was a woman's voice.

'DCP Kabir,' he said a little pompously. 'Who's speaking?'

'Yes, DCP Kabir. I'm sorry. This is Mrs Sequeira, Sharon's mother, speaking.'

Kabir was all attention. 'Good evening, Mrs Sequeira. How can I help you?'

'I… Do you have any news about my daughter?'

'I'm afraid not, ma'am. But I can assure you that we're doing everything possible to locate her.'

'Could she… be dead?'

Kabir paused. 'I don't know, but let's hope for the best.'

There was silence at the other end.

'Mrs Sequeira?'

'Yes… I'm here.' She sounded broken.

'Do you have any idea where your daughter might be?'

'No, DCP Kabir. I really don't. She's never gone away like this… without telling anyone.'

Kabir didn't say anything to that. *She's never been a murder suspect before either.*

Mrs Sequeira continued, 'My grandson is absolutely distraught. He can't understand why his mother hasn't been home for so many days.'

'Please think, ma'am. Is there anything you know, anything that can help us find Sharon?'

'Oh… I just remembered why I called you.'

'Yes?'

'When you had asked me about Sharon, I told you that she was preoccupied and left in a bit of a hurry that evening.'

'I remember that.'

'But I had forgotten something completely…'

'What?'

'When Sharon came home from the clinic, she immediately asked me about an envelope that had been delivered in the morning. At first, I thought we had thrown it away, and when I told her that, she got angry. But it turned out that my grandson had kept it to doodle on.'

'So it was there?'

'Yes, Sharon found it on his bed. Honestly, I didn't really think much of it at that time. She keeps getting promotional material from companies, dental journals and so on.'

'What was inside the envelope then?'

'Today, I thought I would go through her room and see if there's any clue to where she might have gone. I've never done that, you know. Sharon's an extremely private person, and she would be very upset if she found out.

'The envelope was in her drawer. I opened it, and there were three photographs inside. Again, I hesitated because I realised this had nothing to do with her work.'

Kabir felt a rising excitement. He could sense an important lead coming.

'The photos were of her… boyfriend.'

'Dev Malik?'

'Yes.'

'Go on.'

'The girl with him in the photos…' She stopped.

'Who was it?'

'It… was Rhea. Sharon's friend.'

17

WHEN the maid stood in front of Harry Shah's apartment and rang the doorbell, there was no response as usual. She sighed and rang again, harder this time. It was the same story every morning. The man would eventually open the door in a groggy state, having only woken up upon her arrival, even though it was well past ten o'clock.

However, several minutes went by and Harry didn't emerge. She figured that he was out somewhere and was about to go away when she noticed that the front door was ajar. She pushed it open and walked in.

It was dark inside as all the curtains were drawn. The maid pulled them open, as was her daily ritual, and went towards Harry's bedroom. 'Sahib, are you awake?'

She saw that the bed had been slept in, but there was no one in the room. The air conditioner was still on. The familiar purple pyjamas lay on the floor in a heap. She checked the bathroom, and then the rest of the house. He wasn't in the apartment.

She called the lobby from the intercom. The security guard informed her that he had been on duty since seven o' clock in the morning and hadn't seen Harry. He must have gone out before his shift had started. The maid worried that it was quite abnormal for Harry to have surfaced so early, and left home in such a rush. As slovenly and disorganised as he was, even he wouldn't have left the front door open. *Something must be wrong*, she told herself and went down to inform the building manager.

The night guard was called up, and he said that Harry had left the building before dawn. He wasn't sure of the exact time but guessed it was around five-thirty. Harry had looked dishevelled as if he had just woken up and dressed in a hurry. The gate security confirmed that he had driven out in his white Mercedes.

There was no evidence of foul play, and the alarm wasn't raised immediately. Despite the maid's apprehensions, the manager felt that it wasn't so unusual for Harry to have gone out early in the morning. After all, he lived alone and could do what he liked. The only problem was that he had no known family, and there was no emergency contact listed in the society records. He wasn't too popular among the building residents either, so not much was known about him.

The manager informed the society chairman, who pulled out Harry's mobile number from their building WhatsApp group and dialled. The phone was switched off. The two of them nevertheless concluded that there was no reason to panic yet. Harry had obviously left home on some urgent work and would return eventually.

The chairman still tried his number a few more times but kept getting the same message. Then in the afternoon, a resident messaged on the WhatsApp group, asking if anyone knew Harry's whereabouts. She had been called by a mutual friend who was supposed to have met Harry for lunch, and not only had he not shown up without any notice but was also unreachable on his mobile, which was very unlike him.

The chairman decided that it was time to inform the police.

The Mercedes was an indulgence Harry could ill-afford, but then, keeping up appearances had always been important to him. Everyone in Ocean West owned luxury cars, and he didn't want to be an exception. He had purchased the second-hand E-Class at a throwaway price from a used-car dealer who was shutting shop.

It was another matter that he hadn't been able to pay any rent for the past three months. The only reason he wasn't thrown out of the apartment was that his father was settling it with the landlord back in Bristol, but that wasn't about to continue for long. Harry had been served an ultimatum by his old man, who knew his son only too well. One more payment and that was going to be it.

After returning to the UK, Harry had spent a few years leading a quiet and uneventful life, by his standards. He set up a store selling ethnic Indian wear, with a supply line from a couple of amateur designers back in Delhi. His father funded the venture of course, not because he thought it was a good commercial proposition, but because he was pleased that his son was finally doing something meaningful. Harry had mentioned to him vaguely that he had gained some experience in apparel trade back in India, though not the fact that it was in the completely illegal business of luxury fakes.

The store did well at first, becoming more popular with English buyers than the South Asian population Harry targeted. The children's line was especially in demand, with frequent bulk orders for return gifts at birthday parties or for festivals and weddings. However, while Harry could apply a big markup on what he paid for the clothes, the overall business wasn't that profitable, after accounting for real estate, logistics and other costs. The only way to make it big was to increase the number of outlets and expand to other cities, but Harry knew it would be too much work. And honest work at that, for it was far more difficult to cut corners in England than in India. For starters, it was next to impossible to bribe any official without a big risk of getting caught.

In the meantime, the designers began to demand a larger share of the margins, which Harry wasn't agreeable to, and they quit in a huff one day. He replaced them with a small manufacturer in Mumbai who supplied the street markets of Bandra and Colaba. While he was cheaper, the clothes were mass-produced and not nearly as fetching as the handmade, limited-edition items Harry's patrons had gotten used to. The store's revenues started to decline, and when it eventually slipped into the red, Harry decided to close down. He had become bored of it anyway.

For the next couple of years, Harry worked in the family business, establishing their first store outside Bristol, in the Midlands city of Birmingham, just a two-hour drive away. He wasn't particularly happy subsisting on what amounted to an allowance from his father, but there was nothing better to do. He certainly wouldn't get a job anywhere, not that he particularly wanted to work nine to five for any company. He bided his time, waiting for the elusive break that would make him rich again.

What helped Harry during this period was a passionate relationship with a Sri Lankan schoolmate who had just broken out of a loveless marriage. They had met at a school reunion after many years, and it didn't take Harry long to recognise and then awaken the hidden desires in his old friend. It was liberating for Harry to be open about his sexual orientation without fear, unlike in India where it would invite derision, prejudice, and even abuse.

But Harry still missed India and longed to get back there. He missed the chaos and unpredictability, the street food and Old Monk, and the warmth of the people. Having lived in both countries, he had come to the bitter conclusion that the colour of one's skin mattered. A lot. His family had been settled in England for decades and assimilated well into the local society and culture, but they would forever remain outsiders. Whereas in India, despite being a misfit in many ways, there was never a moment when Harry didn't feel completely at home.

One day, Harry's mother put him in touch with a distant cousin, who lived in Mumbai and was visiting Bristol, and asked him to help her. She was an ad film-maker, and had just got a big break to direct a mainstream Bollywood movie. It was a romance with two young debut actors and set in the UK. She didn't want to film in London because it was already an overwhelming favourite of producers, and the familiar London Eye-dominated cityscape was the opening backdrop of too many Indian movies. Instead, she chose Bristol, for its hilly topography, distinctive buildings and bridges, and proximity to the ancient city of Bath.

Harry was happy with the diversion, and for the next few days, he showed her around as she scouted for shooting locations, made enquiries about casting agencies, and applied for permissions required from the city authorities. When the filming finally began, Harry spent a lot of time on the sets and became a local consultant-cum-host for his cousin and her crew. The movie went on to become a big hit, and she was instantly catapulted to the big league. Grateful to Harry for all his help, she asked him to join the new production company she was setting up back in Mumbai.

Harry had thoroughly enjoyed his brush with movie-making, and it was a tempting offer. However, he couldn't forget the menacing face of the man whose money he had run away with and knew that he would be risking his life by returning to India. When he mentioned this to his cousin though, she laughed and told him that there was nothing to worry about, because that particular kingpin had been recently bumped off by a rival in a high-profile daylight shooting, and his gang was disbanded.

Not one to ignore such serendipity, Harry decided that it was finally time for him to return to Mumbai.

When the phone rang just after five o'clock in the morning., Harry was in deep slumber and didn't hear it. Too many rums the previous evening had knocked him out completely. The phone buzzed again, and this time, he woke up with the persistent ringing.

Without noticing the number, Harry took the call and said groggily, 'Hello?'

'I have what you want, but you need to come for it now.'

'Who's... this?'

'You know who this is.'

Harry finally recognised the voice and tried to think through the fog in his head. 'Wha... what's the... time?'

'Do you want it or not?'

'Yes... but...'

'Aarey Colony. New Zealand Hostel. You know where that is?'

'I... can find it. But... right now?'

'Yes. I can't do this later.'

Harry's mind was clearing. 'You forget that you... aren't in a position to dictate anything...'

It was as if he hadn't spoken. The voice was hard, implacable. 'Just get your sorry ass there in half an hour, and call me back on this number when you reach.'

There was a pause. 'And Harry, don't forget to keep your end of the bargain.'

The line went dead.

Harry knew he had no option but to go as directed. He managed to get ready in ten minutes and rushed out with his mobile phone, car keys and a manila envelope. Sunrise was well over an hour away. He punched in the location in Google Maps and was soon racing along the deserted Western Express Highway.

As Harry drove, he began to think more calmly. If the plan had been to surprise him, it had worked admirably. He hadn't expected an early morning call out of the blue, and certainly not so soon. However, he still held all the cards so it didn't really matter. A lucky coincidence had given him the opportunity to solve all his problems for good. It was nothing short of a lifeline, which he had grabbed with both hands. *It's actually better that this gets over quickly, and I can then move on.* Harry's excitement grew as he turned off the Highway towards Aarey Road.

Aarey Milk Colony is a heavily forested area in the suburb of Goregaon, comprising twelve villages and over thirty cattle farms. It boasts of a rich biodiversity, with an array of wild animals and several species of birds, butterflies and insects. Within its limits is also the famous Film City, an integrated studio complex where many Bollywood films have been shot, at least in the days before budgets allowed more exotic locales.

The road Harry drove on cut right through Aarey Colony all the way to Powai, with dense greenery on both sides for most of its length. He passed a small lake, a picnic area and some scattered buildings before pulling up in front of his destination. The New Zealand Hostel is a student dormitory, and the large, drab monolith stands at the intersection of the Aarey Road and a narrow lane popular with joggers and cyclists.

Harry stepped out of the car. It was quite dark, with the only illumination coming from a dim light atop one of the gateposts of the hostel. He took out his phone and saw a message: 'Cross the main road and keep walking through the trees.' He dialled the number, but there was no response. Harry suddenly felt a stab of fear. There wasn't a soul around, and it was deathly quiet. Not even a bird chirped. He knew that Aarey was home to leopards, and there had been cases of attacks on humans. What he didn't know was that the exact spot where he stood was rumoured to be haunted.

He switched on the torch in his mobile phone and hesitantly crossed the road. There was a wall of darkness in front of him. He stopped. *Something's not right. I understand the need for secrecy, but why this place?* Ignoring the cautionary voice inside his head and driven by greed, Harry stepped into the undergrowth.

As he took the first fearful steps, there was a rustling noise behind and he whirled around, flashing the torch from left to right. He could only see the trees and bushes bathed in the eerie, white glow. It was cool, but sweat poured down his face. He turned and continued. A few seconds later, he heard the same noise, closer this time.

Before he could react, there was a terrible blow to the back of his head and he knew no more.

18

NUSRAT stared at her laptop screen and frowned.

On Kabir's instructions, she had been probing Dev's background, trying to shed some new light on the case. In the past, that would have meant a lot of legwork and the slow, painstaking process of locating and interviewing each contact of the victim individually. In the age of social media though, she could reach out to his entire network of friends and family sitting at her desk.

Nusrat found out plenty of information about Dev. He had kept loose privacy settings on his accounts. So it was quite easy, in fact. She already had his phone contacts and recent messages. However, it all added up to his known persona and there was nothing useful she could take to Kabir.

Until the cryptic new message she received that morning from one of Dev's Sanawar buddies. He was among the minority of men in Dev's close circle of friends, and the last to respond to her.

He had written, 'Hope you are investigating his wife. This is not the first time this has happened. Check the case of Sunny Gupta. He supposedly committed suicide. Tanya was his girlfriend, then.'

Nusrat googled the name and was flooded with results, none of whom seemed to have committed suicide. She pulled out her mobile and dialled SI Patil.

'Sir, this is Nusrat.'

'Good morning.'

'Do you recall any case of a Sunny Gupta? It was a suicide. Probably some years back.'

The name rang a bell. Patil tried to jog his memory. 'Sunny Gupta… Sunny Gupta… Where have I heard that name?'

Nusrat waited.

'Ah yes. Now I remember. A Delhi boy. He fell off the roof of a building in Versova…'

'You worked on the case, sir?'

'No. I was posted in Aurangabad at that time. But the house belonged to a film producer for whom we had once done a protection detail after he received an extortion threat. I soon figured that it was a bogus call made by one of his disgruntled employees, and he was very grateful. In fact, when this boy fell, the producer first called me. The incident happened at his son's birthday party.'

'That's a real coincidence. How long back was this?'

'Let me see… At least ten years, if not more. But what is this about, Nusrat?'

She told him about the email from Dev's friend.

'Is he implying that Tanya had something to do with Sunny's death?'

'I guess so, sir.'

'Hmm... I didn't know she was there that night. The story was that Sunny was depressed and decided to take his own life. He was also very drunk.'

'Was there an investigation?'

'Well, any accidental death has to be investigated, of course. In this case, I think foul play was ruled out pretty quickly. The boy was alone on the roof when it happened.'

'Was Tanya questioned, sir?'

'I wouldn't know. The records will be at Versova thana somewhere.'

'Thanks. I'll try that.'

'Nusrat, you think Dev was murdered by his wife?'

'I don't know, sir. But we need to explore this angle.'

'She has a solid alibi. That's the first thing we checked.'

'The spouse is always a suspect, right?'

After hanging up, Nusrat replied to Dev's friend, asking for more details. She was especially keen to know how he had heard about the incident. *Had Dev told him? Or had he known Sunny himself?* She knew it was a long shot. From what Patil had said, there was no reason to believe Tanya had anything to do with Sunny's death. And yet, it was uncanny that such a link had suddenly come up.

Nusrat decided to pay Tanya a visit. She debated whether to tell Kabir but figured she would wait to get something more concrete. *I may not be a detective, but I can still follow up a lead and help the case.*

At that moment, Kabir was sitting across an agitated Rhea Menon. He had visited Mrs Sequeira early in the morning and picked up the envelope with the photos.

'Where were these taken exactly?' Kabir asked.

He had laid out the photos on the table between them. They showed Dev and Rhea sitting in a restaurant, having dinner. In one shot, Dev appeared to have his hand on hers and in another, they were clinking wine glasses. It all looked very romantic.

'We... were at Gaylord. In Churchgate.' Kabir was thinking that the place seemed familiar. It was one of south Mumbai's iconic restaurants, and he loved their old-style Continental food. He made a mental note to go there for lunch soon.

Rhea continued, 'I assure you, DCP Kabir, there was nothing going on between Dev and me. He was buying a birthday gift for Shar and... wanted some advice. That's all.'

'He could have called you. Why the dinner?'

'He had decided on pashmina. It's the old state emporiums and the five-star hotel stores that have the best, genuine stuff, and I went along to help him choose. He didn't want to go wrong because Shar is very finicky. When we were finally done, Dev suggested dinner and I agreed. Gaylord was nearby so we went there.'

Kabir had bought his wife a pashmina scarf some years ago, which had cost him half a month's salary, and he had done the same circuit back then. The story sounded plausible. And even if it wasn't true, adultery wasn't a crime by itself any more.

'How well did you know Dev?'

'Only through Shar. Apart from the dinner that evening, I met him a few times at her apartment and at parties. But never alone.'

'Do you know who might have clicked these photographs?'

Rhea thought for a moment. 'It was a weekday evening. But the restaurant was crowded, I recall. It could have been anyone. I'm sure there was no one there that either of us knew.'

'In the photos, both of you look quite intimate, wouldn't you say?'

Rhea sighed. 'Dev was an extremely attractive man, and he really turned on the charm that evening. He knew how close Shar and I were, like sisters practically. Maybe I got a little carried away. It was just harmless flirting though, nothing more.'

'Did he proposition you?'

She stared at him. 'No, of course not. He was completely in love with her.'

'I wouldn't blame Sharon if she concluded from these photos that Dev was cheating on her with her best friend. Especially given his reputation,' Kabir said.

Rhea nodded. 'She was insanely possessive of him. I've never seen her like that before. I think she had psyched herself up that he would be unfaithful to her one day or another, and was desperate to stop that from happening.'

Kabir suddenly wondered if his wife had ever cheated on him. She was attractive and successful, and all her travel meant that the opportunity was always there. Besides, their marriage wasn't that great any more. *If I ever catch her with another man, I'll kill him,* he thought grimly.

He asked, 'Where did you go after dinner with Dev?'

'He dropped me home, that's all.'

'Your husband knows about it?'

Rhea looked uncomfortable. 'He was out of town that day. I don't think he would mind anyway. He's aware that many of my friends are men.'

'So you didn't tell him?'

'Well… no.'

Tears welled up in her eyes. 'I feel awful about this. Shar must have been so terribly upset seeing the photos. Why didn't she just call me?'

'You spoke to her earlier that day, right?'

'Yes, she sounded worried because of the call from the woman but was quite normal with me. I guess she hadn't seen the photos then.'

'Did she mention the envelope?'

'No, I'm pretty sure she didn't. The first I heard about it was from you.'

Kabir stood up. 'All right. If you think of anything else, call me.'

Rhea said hesitantly, 'DCP Kabir, do you think… Shar might have killed Dev in a fit of jealousy?'

'It's an angle we've been exploring. These photos certainly strengthen that theory.'

The man was taking his usual shortcut through the forest. He lived in a hamlet inside Aarey Colony and worked as a driver in one of the adjoining high-rises. The sun was already high in the sky, but he was in no hurry. His employers were on vacation, and all he had to do was check on the car every couple of days. He was nearing the main Aarey Road when the persistent cawing of crows behind a bush attracted his attention.

Normally, he would have ignored it, but something made him go and investigate. The birds were pecking at a dark shape under a layer of dry leaves. As he got closer, the smell of decaying flesh hit him like a wave. Seeing him, some of the crows flew away to a nearby tree while the others remained on the ground a few feet away, clearly reluctant to abandon their meal.

The man figured that the carcass was too big to be a dog. *Was it a leopard kill?* He looked around fearfully, wishing he wasn't alone. Some irresistible impulse kept him going until he stood next to what he suddenly realised was a human shape. The blanched, lifeless face staring up at him through the shroud of leaves confirmed it. One eye was open, and the other had been gouged out.

The man screamed and sank to the ground. For a few seconds, he was unable to move, mesmerised by the ghastly sight. Then he managed to scramble away, get up on shaky legs, and stumble towards the road. Behind him, the crows resumed their feast.

Within thirty minutes, a jeep from the Aarey police station and a rickety ambulance arrived at the scene. The victim was beyond any medical help, of course. The back of his head had been bashed in with a blunt object. There was no identification on his body, and his mobile was missing.

The police inspector and two constables did a preliminary search of the area, but there wasn't much to find in all the undergrowth. It appeared that the man had been killed at the same spot, not more than a few hours ago. From his clothes, they deduced that he was well-to-do. A small crowd had gathered and watched with morbid fascination as the body was wrapped in a coarse sheet and loaded into the ambulance on a rusted metal stretcher.

Leaving his constables to make further enquiries, the inspector got into his jeep and was about to drive away, when he noticed the white Mercedes across the road. It was unusual for any vehicle to be parked there at that hour, so he stopped to check it out. The doors were locked, and there was no one inside. The security guard of the New Zealand Hostel informed him that the Mercedes had been at the same spot since the time he had reported for duty early in the morning. He hadn't seen anyone get in or out of it.

There didn't remain any further doubt that the car belonged to the victim. The inspector noted down the licence plate number and called the traffic control room. A quick check on the database revealed that the vehicle was registered in the name of what appeared to be a shell company. Convinced that the dead man must be rich or influential, the inspector immediately notified the Missing Persons Bureau, the centralised unit under the Crime Branch.

When the society chairman of Ocean West reported Harry Shah missing, his description of Harry's car lit up an immediate match with the circular received from Aarey that morning. The young girl on duty noted the address and duly placed a call to the Worli thana.

SI Patil was laboriously typing out a report on his desktop when a constable burst into his chamber excitedly.

He looked up, annoyed at the abrupt intrusion. 'Yes, what is it?'

'Sir, we have another murder in Ocean West!'

'What?'

'The victim's name is Haribhai Shah. He lived in the apartment just below Dev Malik's.'

Patil pushed away the keyboard and took off his spectacles. 'Tell me what happened.'

Ten minutes later, he picked up his phone and dialled Kabir.

19

TANYA stood with her arms crossed, a determined expression on her face. She was wearing a black, fitted jumpsuit which accentuated her long limbs perfectly. Her hair was tied in a dark bandana, and a pair of large sunglasses completed the stealth look.

She was on the top floor of an unfinished building in Powai. There was plenty of litter around, pieces of concrete, empty cartons, plastic bags, screws, wires, beer cans, cigarette butts and a broken chair. The pillars had been erected, but there were no walls. Tanya could see verdant hills and a clutch of high-rises in the distance. Construction had stopped years ago after the builder ran into financial trouble, and the entire property had fallen into a long-drawn and bitter litigation.

A blue Maruti Swift drove up the ramp and stopped near Tanya. The driver's door opened, and a man stepped out. He was wearing a white shirt left untucked over navy blue trousers, and a pair of walking sandals. He looked middle aged and middle class, and could have been anything from a schoolteacher to a bank employee. There was an old-style briefcase in his hand.

Tanya asked tersely, 'Do you have it?'

The man looked around nervously. 'Yes, here it is.'

She took the briefcase from him and opened it. 'Who uses these nowadays?'

He waited for her to examine the contents.

Satisfied, Tanya turned back to him. 'If I find out later that anything is missing, you know the consequences.'

'Don't worry, ma'am. It's all there.'

'Does anyone know you're here?'

'No, I don't think so.'

'What about your boss?'

'I told him I'm sick.'

She moved closer to him. 'And you won't tell anyone about this, I hope?'

The man smiled weakly. 'How can I, ma'am?'

The knife in Tanya's hand gleamed briefly before she plunged it into his chest. His face contorted in shock and pain, and there was an audible sigh of air escaping from his lungs. A patch of red bloomed rapidly on his white shirt. She pulled out the knife and stabbed him again. This time, he groaned and collapsed to the ground.

Tanya lifted her sunglasses to her forehead and watched calmly as he twitched for a few seconds and then lay still. Her eyes were cold and remorseless.

'I still had to make sure,' she whispered to the dead man and walked away.

'Cut!' The voice of the director boomed. 'Let's take a thirty-minute break, folks.'

Tanya turned and smiled. 'How was it?'

'A perfect shot.'

The 'dead man' got up and dusted himself. 'I'm a real mess,' he muttered.

Tanya patted him on the back and walked over to where Nusrat was sitting.

The two women shook hands. Nusrat began, 'Thank you for meeting me.'

She had initially planned to just land up at Tanya's apartment in the evening because it was never a good idea to let a potential suspect know in advance that the police were coming to ask questions. However, she realised that given Tanya's shooting schedules, there was a strong possibility she wouldn't be home. So she called and set up the appointment.

Tanya gave Nusrat an appraising look, and said, 'Today's a crazy day. I thought it's best we meet here.'

'Interesting scene. It's a web series, I gather?'

'That's the future, you know. Television and even films are going to become passé.'

'You were very convincing. For a moment, I thought you actually killed him.' Nusrat pointed to a red streak on the back of Tanya's hand. 'Even that blood looks so real.'

'*That* is real blood. I cut myself yesterday.' She made no move to wipe it off and narrowed her eyes. 'I thought DCP Kabir was handling Dev's case. Why isn't he here?'

'I'm part of his investigation team,' said Nusrat smoothly. 'Do you remember Sunny Gupta?'

There was a flicker of surprise in Tanya's eyes. 'Sunny? Yes… That was long back.'

'You dated him?'

'Briefly. We were both newcomers.'

'Do you remember the night of his death?'

'How could I forget? It was so tragic. Sunny was struggling to get a break and was totally depressed.'

'Were you with him when he jumped?'

'No, I wasn't.' Tanya's face hardened. 'I assume you must know that?'

'Well, there's still some doubt about the exact sequence of events.'

'Sunny committed suicide. The police report clearly said that. Where's the doubt?'

Nusrat pulled out a notebook and opened it. 'Multiple witnesses said that you had a big fight with Sunny at the party. What was it about?'

'Yes... we did. In fact, I broke up with him that evening.'

'Why?'

'I caught him cheating, Nusrat.' There was a strange look in Tanya's eyes. 'What would you have done?'

'Do you think the break-up might have sent him over the edge? No pun intended, of course.'

Tanya sighed. 'I don't know. Sunny was a very temperamental guy. Moody but impulsive. That night, he had drunk too much and was barely able to stand straight.'

'Where were you exactly when he jumped?' Nusrat didn't mention that as per the case file one guest had initially said he saw Tanya running down from the terrace after the incident, but later, he retracted his statement.

'Where are you going with this?' Tanya's voice rose a few decibels. 'Are you saying I had something to do with Sunny's death?'

'Please answer the question.'

'Look, I don't exactly remember. I wasn't fully sober myself, and it was so many years ago. The bungalow was huge. I think I was sitting somewhere by myself, trying to clear my head. Most of the people had left by then. Someone suddenly screamed, and I rushed out along with whoever else was around.'

Nusrat wasn't sure whether to believe Tanya but remained silent. Surprisingly, there was no statement from her recorded in the case file. Either it had been removed or she hadn't been questioned, both of which were equally suspicious.

'Is there anything else?' Tanya looked at the Omega Constellation on her wrist. 'I need to go now.'

'Where were you the night Dev was murdered?'

'I was at home all evening, my dear, as I've already told your bosses. Feel free to check my alibi again, if you've nothing better to do.'

'I will, thank you.' Nusrat got up.

'Stop wasting your time here, and focus on finding Dev's killer.' Nusrat resisted the temptation to snap back at her patronising tone and walked off.

It had been six frustrating months before Tanya finally got her first audition call from the casting director of an upcoming Bollywood film. She took the next flight to Mumbai and landed up at the man's Bandra office at the appointed time. But after waiting for two hours, she was told that he was not coming in and had asked her to meet him at his apartment.

Tanya's antennae were immediately on alert, but she had no option other than to go. When the door opened though, she realised that she needn't have worried. The man was quite obviously gay. He asked a few perfunctory questions and made her read some lines from a much-thumbed dummy script. But she wasn't sure he even listened because he kept typing away on his phone throughout. At the end, he looked up and stared at her speculatively.

She asked, 'Well, what do you think?'

'Think of what?'

'My... reading. The audition.'

'Oh darling, nobody cares about that.' He waved his hands in an affected manner. 'I only need to see if you'll fit the part physically.'

'And do I?'

'You're a little too tall, but you'll do.'

Tanya's heart leapt. 'So I get the part?'

'Not so soon, dear.' He sighed. 'This is your first time, isn't it?'

'Yes, you know that.'

'You'll need to meet the director. He... er... needs to be happy with you as well.'

'What do you mean exactly?'

He looked her up and down. 'You're his type, so I think it'll be fine. Can you meet him tonight?'

Tanya had heard about the casting couch, of course, but it still didn't make his words any less unpleasant. She knew it was a prominent, big-budget film, and she had the opportunity to grab a small but important role in it. The director was reputed to have the Midas touch, having delivered back-to-back hits recently. It would be the perfect launch pad for her.

Seeing her hesitation, the man said, 'Don't overthink it, dear. A girl's got to do what she's got to do to get ahead in this world. Don't I know it myself?' He rolled his eyes.

The doorbell rang, and he perked up visibly. 'You can go now. Let me know your decision by the afternoon. There's a long queue, if you aren't interested.'

As she walked out, she had a good look at the new visitor. He was tall and rugged-looking but dressed shabbily.

As it happened, Tanya didn't get the role, but in the meantime, she was approached by a major television studio to replace one of the lead actors in an ongoing series. It was a long-running, successful show but in urgent need of a reboot with new faces. The producer was anyway tired of the tantrums of her main cast, and she wanted to prove to them that no one was indispensable.

Tanya couldn't have asked for a better start to her career. She turned out to be terrific in the role of an erudite, scheming woman who had returned from abroad and laid a claim to the fortune of the family at the centre of the drama, revealing a relationship with the patriarch that had remained hidden for years. She instantly connected with the primarily middle-class audience of the serial, who waited for eight o'clock every evening with bated breath to find out what her next machinations were going to be.

At a party to celebrate the resurgence of the show, Tanya met the man she had seen at the casting director's apartment. He wasn't invited but had bribed his way in, knowing there would be important industry people there.

His name was Sunny Gupta, and he had come to the city with good looks and a dream, like countless other hopefuls.

Tanya spotted him and walked over. 'So, did you get the part?'

He recognised her immediately, and said sheepishly, 'Nope. Looks like we both got screwed over by that fag.'

'Yes, indeed.' She laughed and raised her glass of champagne. 'Let's drink to that.'

That night, they ended up in her small Lokhandwala flat. She found his masculine vulnerability attractive, and he needed no encouragement to get into the bed of a newly minted television star. It was the beginning of a passionate but ill-fated relationship.

Tanya had lied to Nusrat about the night of Sunny's death. Neither of them was as drunk as she had claimed, and she had been with him on the terrace when he fell.

20

KABIR shivered as he stared at the corpse of Harry Shah. It wasn't from the sight of the mutilated face, for he had seen far worse, but from the extremely cold temperature of the morgue.

The pathologist had pulled out the deep metal drawer in which the body was kept after the post-mortem. It was bundled in a white sheet, tied around the neck and ankles. The eyes were sewn shut and there was a rough suture along the forehead where the skull had been sawed open. The skin had a ghostly pallor in the dim white light.

Kabir asked, 'What was the cause of death, doctor?'

'Two injuries to the back of his head with a heavy, blunt object. Something made of stone or metal. The first blow cracked the bone, and the second one caved in the skull.'

'Death was instantaneous?'

'I think so. He must have been attacked from behind.'

'Was there an intent to kill or could it have been accidental?'

'Oh, it was definitely intentional. The force of the blows leaves no room for doubt.'

'What about the time of death?'

'I estimate it to be between six and seven in the morning.'

'Sir?' Patil had been standing a few feet behind, his face covered with a large floral handkerchief. He hated morgues, and could barely keep himself from retching at the sickly antiseptic smell. 'It looks like the victim had been called to the spot for a rendezvous by his killer. I doubt he would be going all the way from Worli to Aarey for a morning walk.'

Kabir frowned. 'You're right, Harish. It certainly looks to be premeditated.'

'In fact, in the missing person report filed, it was mentioned that the man never went out anywhere before afternoon. I wonder what it was that made him go there at that hour.'

'Did we get a forensic unit to the crime scene?'

'No, sir. It was too late. The Aarey police did a search of the area but didn't find anything useful.'

'Ask them to send someone to the spot early tomorrow morning, and question the morning walkers. One of them might have seen or heard something.'

'Yes, sir.'

Kabir turned back to the pathologist. 'Anything else from the post-mortem?'

'I'm waiting for the viscera analysis. All I can tell you is that the man was a heavy drinker. His liver was in terrible shape.'

'What about his clothes?'

'I've sent them to the lab.'

Kabir nodded. 'Thank you, doctor. Come, Harish. I think we're done here.'

'There's one more thing I should mention.'

'What's that?'

'I found a couple of strands of hair on the man's neck. They weren't his own.'

'So it could be the killer's?'

'Possibly. I bagged them separately and recommended a DNA analysis.'

Patil said, 'Maybe the killer bent down over the victim to make sure he was dead, and shed his hair unknowingly?'

'You're right, except for one thing. I think that hair likely came from a woman.'

Kabir took a handful of makhana and pushed the bowl towards Patil. They were back at the Crime Branch headquarters after the visit to JJ Hospital.

'Have some makhana, Harish. Roasted fox nuts. It's a very healthy snack. Your wife will approve.'

Patil helped himself, and said, 'Thank you, sir. I've only seen this being sold on flights.'

'I've also decided to watch my calories, you know.'

Patil grinned. 'Ah, madam has finally managed to get you under her control.'

Kabir smiled briefly but didn't respond. Truth was, his wife wasn't particularly bothered about what he was eating, and certainly too busy to think about getting him on a diet.

He asked, 'So, what do we know about Harry Shah?'

'It appears that he was quite a dubious character, sir.' Patil handed him a slim folder. 'I just got this from the Economic Offences Wing. They were tracking him in connection with a cheating scam at a cooperative bank. He was suspected to be some kind of a go-between.'

Kabir read the summary report on Harry. 'It's a wonder the man has never been arrested. He's been involved in so many illegal businesses—gambling, counterfeiting, betting, hawala. And now bank fraud to top it all.'

'Yes, sir. Harry Shah was a smart operator. Somehow, he always stayed one step ahead of the law.'

'He had no family here, I believe?'

'He lived alone. We've informed his parents in Bristol, England. His father is reaching Mumbai tonight.'

'What about friends?'

'We're still making enquiries, sir. It seems Harry wasn't very social or popular. His network was mostly in shady circles. Unfortunately, his mobile is missing.' Patil rolled his eyes. 'I wish these murderers had the basic manners to leave their victim's phone behind so that our job was a little easier.'

Kabir leaned forward. 'And he was Dev Malik's neighbour.'

'We had questioned him after Dev's murder, but he said that he hadn't seen or heard anything.'

'Where was he that night?'

'At home. No alibi.'

'How well did he know Dev?'

'That's the thing, sir.' Patil frowned. 'He told us that he didn't know Dev well, but we're hearing a different story now. The strong rumour in the society is that something apparently happened between the two men, and they disliked each other.'

'That's interesting.' Kabir looked thoughtful. 'Do we know what exactly happened?'

'No, but I can tell you something even more interesting.' Patil smiled triumphantly. 'Harry Shah was homosexual.'

Kabir exclaimed, 'I simply can't imagine Dev Malik sleeping with a man!'

'You never know, sir. Maybe he wanted to experiment.'

Just then, Nusrat entered. 'Who's experimenting with what?'

Kabir looked up at her and pointed towards Patil. 'Harish will tell you.'

'The Harry Shah case, sir?'

Patil narrated what Kabir and he were discussing.

'It's quite possible,' Nusrat said confidently. 'If Harry was gay, he must have been attracted to Dev. That man was such a stunner. We'll probably never know if anything actually happened between them, but I wouldn't be surprised if it did. Bisexuality is far more common than you think, both among men and women.'

Kabir still looked sceptical. 'And how would you know about that, Nusrat?'

She smiled enigmatically at him but didn't say anything.

'Let's assume you're right. How does that link the two murders?'

'If Harry was jilted by Dev, that could have been his motive.'

Kabir shook his head. 'Somehow, I don't see Harry Shah as a murderer. He was a crooked man but a careful one. A crime of passion so close to home doesn't seem his style.'

'Passion leads people to do strange things, doesn't it?' Nusrat stared at him intently. 'Not everyone has your self-control, sir.'

Kabir avoided her gaze. 'Anyway, we need to examine all possibilities. Including the one where both Dev and Harry were killed by the same person.'

Patil asked, 'You mean Sharon Sequeira, sir?'

'Possibly. We've now established a strong motive that could have driven her to murder Dev.'

'And the hair found on Harry Shah's body during the post-mortem belongs to a woman.'

Nusrat interjected, 'Really?'

'Yes, that's what the pathologist just told us.' Patil sighed. 'Of course, it's equally possible that there's no connection between the two murders. Harry Shah must have had many enemies and any one of them could be the perpetrator.'

Nusrat smirked. 'Maybe a jealous wife?'

'I don't think so.' Kabir rubbed his nose. 'The timing is too much of a coincidence. Something tells me there's definitely a connection. We need to quickly find out what it is.'

'By the way,' Nusrat piped up. 'I went to meet Tanya today.'

The two men stared at her.

'That's what I came to tell you,' she said defensively. 'Patil Sir, you remember I spoke to you about the Sunny Gupta case?'

Kabir looked quizzical. 'What case is that?'

'Sunny was an old boyfriend of Tanya's, from when she was starting out as an actress. They had gone to a party one evening, and he died mysteriously by falling off the roof of the building where the party was being held. It was ruled a suicide back then, but I have a suspicion she may have pushed him.'

'So you went to question her about that?'

'Yes, sir. One of Dev's friends wrote to me about this incident so I thought I should follow up.'

'And what did you find out?'

'Tanya's an extremely smart woman.' *Not to mention a bloody bitch.* 'Certainly not the bimbo you would expect, and...'

Patil interrupted. 'Yes, beauty and brains.'

Kabir chuckled. 'We have her biggest fan right here.'

Nusrat gave Patil a pained look. 'Sir, she's a very different person from what you see on screen.'

'When we met her at Dev's apartment, she seemed quite normal. Very upset with her husband's death, of course.'

'Well, she's back to shooting less than a week later.' Nusrat sneered. 'She hardly looked like a grieving widow on the sets today.'

Kabir said impatiently, 'What's your point, Nusrat?'

'Sir, all I'm saying is that if she's done it once, maybe she can do it again.'

'Where's the proof that she murdered Sunny Gupta?'

Nusrat said defiantly, 'I don't have proof, but my instinct tells me I'm right.'

'Cases can't be investigated only on instinct, you know that. We need evidence, Nusrat.'

'If we could reopen the case and interview the witnesses again, I'm sure we'll find something, sir.'

'You know we can't do that.'

'I have a strong feeling that things were hushed up.' Nusrat sounded adamant. 'Sunny Gupta was a nobody, one of the thousands of wannabe stars who wash up on the shores of our entertainment industry every year. But Tanya had already become a popular actress in a superhit serial by then, so she had to be protected. That's the way it works in Tinseltown, isn't it?'

'I already told you about the case, Nusrat. It was clearly a suicide, no doubt about that,' said Patil with some irritation. 'And in any event, Tanya has a solid alibi for the night of Dev Malik's murder.'

'Can we rely only on her boyfriend's statement? Maybe he's telling us whatever she wants him to.'

'What could be her motive? She was already separated from Dev, and doesn't need his money either.'

'I… don't know.' She paused. 'But I can tell you that the woman is capable of anything, with or without motive.'

Kabir chimed in, 'Nusrat, it's never easy to rule out the spouse as a suspect in any murder. But I have to agree with Harish… Even if Tanya is psychotic, as you're implying, how could she have got to Dev's apartment that night without being seen? After all, she's a familiar face, especially in that building.'

'You're right, sir. That's something I can't figure out either.'

Just then, Kabir's phone rang. He took the call and hardly spoke during the brief conversation but looked visibly excited.

'I knew it!' He slapped the desk. 'I had asked for Harry Shah's fingerprints to be compared against the unidentified handprint we had found in Dev's apartment and guess what? It's a perfect match.'

21

IRFAN Shaikh was angry. In fact, his anger had been simmering for over a week. He had been so close to getting what he wanted, but fate had played a cruel hand at the last moment.

Irfan was born in a village fifty kilometres from Srinagar and grew up in near poverty. His father was an alcoholic and had abandoned the family when Irfan was just a few months old, leaving his mother to bring up the three children single-handedly. She struggled to eke out a subsistence, working in the apple orchards during harvest time, making the two-hour bus journey to the capital every day during the summer months to cook at one of the hotels, and knitting shawls at home in between.

All the siblings were enrolled in the district primary school, but Irfan regularly played truant. His mother was barely able to feed the family, and she had no time to focus on the children's upbringing. Irfan went astray quickly, getting caught for stealing at the age of ten, knocking out the front teeth of another boy a year later, and molesting their neighbour's daughter when he was just fourteen.

His mother was summoned by the pradhan, who threatened to throw her out of the village if Irfan's behaviour wasn't checked. She begged him for forgiveness and gave the boy a sound thrashing. But she somehow knew that her son was already beyond redemption. For a while, things were calm. Irfan attended school every day and seemed to have become unusually quiet. He was away from home for long periods of time, but there were no complaints against him. His mother began to fervently hope that she had been wrong.

Then one day, the police landed up at their door, looking for Irfan. His mother asked tearfully what he had done, and they replied cryptically that he was involved with terrorists. She pleaded that it was impossible, for he was just a boy and he would never do something like that in any case. The men insisted on searching the house and barged in. It didn't take them long to find the country-made gun under Irfan's mattress.

But of the boy, there was no sign. He had already been tipped off that the police were coming for him and decided to run. It was true that he had been recruited by one of the terror outfits that were active in the state. They specialised in spotting disgruntled youth, and Irfan's misdemeanours had put him on their radar early on.

However, after a few months, Irfan realised that there wasn't really any religious or fundamentalist fervour in him. He understood what was happening but couldn't care less. All he wanted was to get out of the spiral of poverty and censure that his life had become. Someone told Irfan that Mumbai was the city of opportunity, where anything was possible, so he made up his mind to go there.

He stole some money and before the police could catch up with him, he had taken a bus to Jammu and boarded the Swaraj Express to the megapolis. Irfan knew that they wouldn't follow him out of the state, for he hadn't committed any crime yet and they had enough to handle anyway. Since he was still a minor, he figured that with a little bit of luck, he wouldn't even feature in the police records and could make a clean start in a new place.

A man on the train befriended Irfan, seeing that the boy was alone and troubled. He happened to be a trader, carrying shawls, spices and handicrafts to the metros and selling them to the emporiums and boutiques who were always looking for good bargains. Hearing Irfan's story, he said that he knew someone who ran a security agency in Mumbai and could give him a job without asking for any documents. Though not yet an adult, Irfan was broad and squat, with a heavy five-o'clock shadow, and could definitely look the part.

Irfan was initially dubious at the suggestion. He had planned on bigger and better things for himself. Seeing his hesitation, the man told him in no uncertain terms that a big city was very different from his village in the mountains. It was a ruthless jungle, where you had to first learn to survive before thinking of anything else. Irfan slowly realised that meeting this man was indeed a stroke of luck. He had practically got a job even before the train pulled into Bandra Terminus.

Six months later, Irfan found himself working as a security guard in Ocean West.

Neena Razdan met Irfan for the first time when he had come up to her apartment to get a society notice signed. From his looks and accent, she gathered that he was from Kashmir and offered him a cup of the kahwa she had just made. He accepted gratefully and told her how much he missed home. It wasn't strictly true for he was both happy and relieved to have escaped from his miserable village, but he wanted to ingratiate himself with this kind and desirable woman.

Neena pulled out a *morha* for him, and Irfan watched her walking around the house as he sipped on the kahwa. She was wearing a cotton dress, and he could see the outline of her body whenever she moved against the sunlight. His loins stirred, reminding him that he had been celibate for too long. Ever since he had landed up in Mumbai, Irfan had forced himself to be very careful when it came to girls. There wasn't enough money for prostitutes either.

Suddenly, Neena turned towards him and asked, 'What made you leave Kashmir and come here?'

Irfan realised he had been gaping at her and looked away. He said, 'I… My family was very poor… so I thought I would find… some work in a big city.'

'Hmm, I see. Most of the others I've known were running away from… trouble.'

Irfan stared at the floor, wondering whether she had somehow found out about his misdeeds.

She continued, 'You're too young for all that, of course.'

'Yes, madam.'

He smiled nervously, thanked her and left.

After that, Irfan made it a point to stand up and greet Neena with extra enthusiasm whenever she passed the lobby desk, but she rarely acknowledged him. He went up to her apartment a few more times on various pretexts, hoping for another cup of kahwa, but she didn't offer him again. By then, he had already heard about her moods and tantrums, so it wasn't a big surprise.

One evening, after his shift was over, Irfan left the building and was walking to the bus stop when he saw Neena in the distance, standing next to an autorickshaw and arguing loudly with the driver sitting inside. Even as Irfan approached, the man leapt out and wagged a thick finger in her face, shouting obscenities. Neena gave him a resounding slap and in response, he pushed her so hard that she fell to the ground. A couple of passers-by had stopped to stare, but no one intervened.

By then, Irfan had reached the spot. He put a firm hand on the man's shoulder from behind, jerked him around and said angrily, 'What do you think you're doing?'

The man shoved him back and screamed, 'Get lost, boy. This is none of your business.'

Irfan swung a roundhouse punch at him, and it happened to land squarely on the jaw. The much bigger man hadn't been expecting it, and he went down on his knees. Irfan lashed out blindly with his size-ten military-style boots until his adversary was prostrate and motionless from the crushing kicks to his head and sides.

Through his haze of fury, he heard a voice. 'Stop, Irfan. Stop! You'll kill him!'

It was Neena. She had picked herself up and was trying to pull him away. When he turned towards her, his eyes were blazing. She was taken aback at the maniacal look on his face.

'Come, Irfan. Let's go now.' She led him back towards the building. 'You can't stay out here. That man's friends may come for you. These auto drivers all stand up for each other.'

'I'm not scared of anyone,' said Irfan grimly. 'How dare that bastard touch you? You shouldn't have stopped me.'

'And you would have killed him, then what? The police will arrest you and put you in jail. You want that?'

Irfan blurted out, 'Madam, the police couldn't catch me in Kashmir. They won't be able to here either.'

Neena gave him an appraising look but didn't say anything. She asked him to come up to her apartment and made him a cup of kahwa for the much-awaited second time.

'Thank you, Irfan,' she said. 'If you hadn't arrived, I don't know what that man would have done to me. All because I realised that his meter was rigged and refused to pay the inflated fare.'

'It's my job, madam.'

Neena smiled. 'No, it's not. You could have easily walked away.'

'How could I do that, especially after you've been so nice to me?'

'Anyway Irfan, what was that about you running from the police in Kashmir?'

He avoided her penetrating gaze. 'I really shouldn't have said that, madam.'

'But you did say it,' Neena persisted. 'Were you involved with terrorists?'

Irfan sighed. On an impulse, he told her everything. From his difficult childhood and progressive offences to his brush with extremism and the journey to Mumbai.

Neena listened intently. At the end, she said, 'You've certainly had an interesting time, Irfan.'

'That's true. But now, all I want is to make some money and lead a proper life.'

Neena was quiet for a few moments. Then she asked softly, 'If I want you to do something for me, will you do it? I will pay you well, don't worry.'

He looked up at her and replied without hesitation. 'Anything for you, madam.'

Irfan looked at his watch. The night guard was late, as usual. Not that he had anywhere to go particularly. He dialled Neena Razdan's apartment on the intercom.

'Hello?' For a change, she picked it up herself.

'Madam, I really need to speak to you.'

After a pause, she said, 'There's nothing to discuss, Irfan. Stop bothering me.'

Irfan began to say something, but he realised that Neena had already disconnected.

It had been that way ever since that fateful night. When she had first broached the plan with him, he was shocked. Shaking his head, he protested vehemently. 'Madam, have you gone mad? I can't believe what you're saying!'

Neena replied calmly, 'I know exactly what I'm saying, Irfan.'

'But… Why? I mean… There must be some other way.'

'I've thought about it carefully. This is the only way.'

Irfan was quiet, his mind in a tizzy.

She put her hand on his arm. 'You promised to help me.'

'Yes madam, but I never thought it would be something like this!'

'You remember I also told you I would pay you well?'

'How… much?'

His eyes went wide at the figure Neena mentioned.

She continued, 'You'll be set for life, Irfan.'

'I… don't know… what to say, madam.'

She pulled him close, burying his face in her ample bosom. He breathed in her musky scent. 'I've seen the way you look at me, Irfan. Do this job for me, and you won't regret it, I promise.'

That had been two weeks ago.

It was true that Irfan made one small mistake, but it cost him dear. Neena was furious and refused to talk to him after that. There was no sign of the remaining money that was owed to him, though he hadn't yet given up hope of being able to fulfil his burning desire for her.

She owes me that much at least.

The night guard arrived, not a moment too soon for Irfan. He scowled at the older man and went to the basement to change out of his uniform. Suddenly, an idea came to his mind. It was so obvious that he wondered why he hadn't thought of it before.

It was the perfect moment. *She's alone at home now.*

Irfan took the lift up to Neena's apartment. He rang the doorbell and moved away so that he wouldn't be seen through the peephole.

There was a muffled voice. 'Who is it?'

He remained silent.

She opened the door a crack. Irfan immediately put his foot on the jamb and pushed his way inside in a flash.

Neena screamed, not recognising him at first. Then her alarm turned to anger. 'How dare you barge in like this!'

'Madam, I had no other option since you kept avoiding me.'

She stood with her arms akimbo. 'What do you want? I have nothing more to do with you, Irfan.'

'You've cheated me, madam,' he said matter-of-factly. 'I've decided to tell the police everything.'

Neena was quiet for a moment, thinking furiously. Then she said, 'Come inside.' He followed her, and they sat down at the dining table.

'You really think the police will believe you, Irfan? Take your word against mine?'

He put his mobile phone down on the table and said, 'I know how to make them believe me.'

'That I paid you to commit murder?' Neena's voice rose. 'You have no proof.'

Irfan smirked. 'Are you really sure of that, madam?'

She looked uncertain. 'And you think they'll let you go? You're forgetting that you're very much a part of this.'

'They have to catch me first.'

She suddenly grabbed him by the collar. 'You bastard!'

Irfan caught her fists in his large hands and freed himself. He said coolly, 'Abusing me won't help you.'

Neena was immediately contrite. 'I'm… really sorry. I don't know… why I did that.'

'I can understand that you're upset, madam.'

'No.' She shook her head. 'What's done is done.'

'The other man wasn't supposed to be there, you know. It wasn't my fault.'

'That's… been taken care of now.'

'So why don't you pay me the rest of my money, madam? Then I'll keep quiet.'

'You're right, Irfan.' There was a strange expression on Neena's face. 'I think I'll have to do something about that.'

He smiled. 'I hoped you would come around.'

She stood up. 'I'll be right back.'

Neena went to the kitchen and returned after a few minutes with a tray. 'Here, have some tea, Irfan.'

He hesitated for a moment, then accepted the proffered cup. 'Thank you.'

Neena reached her hand out towards him, and he flinched. She caressed his face, smiling. 'You're so strong, so manly. I like that.'

Irfan replied hoarsely, 'I like you a lot too, madam.'

She put her other hand on his thigh. He shivered.

'When have you last been with a girl, Irfan?'

'I… don't remember.'

She took his hands and put them on her breasts. He closed his eyes, moaning softly.

Neena then calmly pulled out the kitchen knife from the waistband of her jeans and plunged it into Irfan.

22

RHEA Menon stared blankly at the hills through the window, tears in her eyes.

She hadn't told Kabir everything about that tryst with Dev. The part about shopping for pashmina was true, and the impromptu dinner as well. He had ordered the most expensive wine in the house, and she ended up drinking too much. As the evening progressed, she became quite intoxicated, as much by Dev as by the alcohol.

When Sharon had started seeing him, Rhea was thoroughly disapproving. She knew her best friend very well, and Dev was absolutely the wrong man for her. But her protests fell on deaf ears, for Sharon was already head over heels in love. She hadn't been in a serious relationship after JP's death, and when Dev entered her life, he had simply blown her away.

Rhea herself was leading a boring domestic life. Her husband was a workaholic, and the passion of their college days had evolved into a comfortable companionship. She spent most of her time looking after their twin girls and the two dogs. They still managed to go for a date night every now and then, but the conversation was rarely romantic, mostly centred around the office and household updates respectively.

That evening at Gaylord, her mind buzzing with alcohol, Rhea felt an uncontrollable desire for Dev. She knew that he found her attractive as well. She was naturally funny and vivacious, and her personal trainer ensured that she was in the best shape of her life. *It's a pity my own husband hasn't noticed.*

When Dev dropped Rhea back, she invited him up to her apartment for coffee. No one else was at home, for Bala had taken the girls to Goa on a long-promised, father–daughters' road trip. As soon as the door closed behind them, she put her arms around his neck and kissed him hard. Dev hesitated, though only for a moment. He was rather drunk himself. They ended up in her bedroom, all thoughts of Sharon forgotten in the throes of wine-induced lust.

The next morning, Rhea woke up to a throbbing hangover and severe pangs of guilt. She couldn't believe that she had just slept with her best friend's boyfriend. *What the hell was I thinking?* She knew that if Sharon found out, she would kill them both. Her temper, though rarely aroused, was scary. And she was crazily jealous of any other woman when it came to Dev.

Both Rhea and Dev agreed that it had been a terrible mistake, a one-night stand that would remain just that. And Sharon could never know about it, of course. They didn't realise then that someone had been following them, and taking photos of them together at Gaylord. The dinner might have been innocuous, as Rhea had sworn to Kabir, but not what happened later.

Sitting locked up in the room, Rhea wondered who had been tailing them that evening. It was possible that some acquaintance of Sharon's might have been there by chance, and spotted them. But then, who was the mystery woman who had called Sharon and presumably sent the photos to her?

Rhea had told Kabir that there was no one whom she knew at the restaurant. In any case, she was so engrossed with Dev after a point that she wouldn't even have noticed. However, something nagged away at her, a faint memory of someone she had seen at Gaylord. Someone who had seemed vaguely familiar but not enough for her to have remembered clearly, and certainly not after all that wine. All she was sure of was that it was a woman, not a man.

The photos hadn't been sent to Bala, and Rhea was thankful for that at least. It meant that the person had no vendetta against her. In the larger scheme of things, it was only a small mercy for he was bound to find out everything soon, though not from her. *Right now, he's probably just worried sick about me.*

Rhea couldn't stop thinking about Sharon. She knew she was in a big mess, and had no one to blame but herself.

When Sharon saw the photos of Rhea with Dev, her first reaction was rage, but then she began to think. The two of them certainly looked intimate, and she could have sworn that neither had mentioned the dinner to her. As far as she knew, Rhea had only met Dev when she was around. *Could I have been there as well?* She racked her memory but couldn't remember any such occasion.

Although Sharon loved Dev with all her heart, the fear of him cheating on her was never far away. He was utterly charming and irresistible, with women throwing themselves at him all the time. In fact, when she started seeing him, it was Rhea who had told her sternly, 'I know Dev's a dreamboat, Shar. Which woman wouldn't want to be with a man like that? But I don't want to see you getting hurt.'

Sharon had ignored her warning for she was completely besotted with Dev. As she looked at the photos again, one part of her refused to believe that Rhea could have done that to her. After all, they were soul sisters. *And was Dev really such a bastard to have cheated on her with her best friend?* Sharon touched the scar on her face, something she always did reflexively when worried or tense.

Suddenly, she remembered Neena Razdan, wondering if she could be the woman who had called her and sent the photos.

Sharon had met that crazy bitch only once, though met was probably not the right word for it. She had just started seeing Dev, not two weeks after the lunch at the farm. He was clearly estranged from his wife, for they lived separately, but he had been evasive about Neena. All he said was that it was over between them, and Sharon hadn't asked anything more.

The fact was Dev had dumped Neena abruptly after meeting Sharon. She had been getting too clingy and was borderline batty, so it was a matter of time anyway.

However, he hadn't dared tell Neena directly, so she was left wondering why he had stopped taking her calls. Not one to let go quietly, Neena stormed up to his apartment one afternoon, something she wouldn't have done earlier without his permission.

When Dev opened the door, she pushed him and barged inside, her eyes blazing. 'What the hell is wrong with you, Dev?' Before he could respond, she noticed Sharon sitting on the sofa.

All hell broke loose. Neena strode up to Sharon and grabbed her by the hair. 'So, this is the bitch you've started bonking, is it?' Shocked, Dev was rooted to his spot for a couple of moments.

Sharon, equally taken aback, recovered first and swung her palm at Neena. The slap struck with a resounding crack, for she was a strong woman. Neena staggered, and Sharon hit her again. By then, Dev had stepped between the two women. He held Neena firmly and shouted, 'You need to leave right now!'

Neena stumbled towards the door, tears streaming down her face. She screamed, 'I'm going to kill both of you!'

The ringing of her mobile phone brought Sharon out of her reverie, and back to the present.

She knew immediately who was calling and said softly, 'Hello?'

There was a terse instruction mentioning a place and time, then the woman hung up.

Sharon had already made up her mind to go, despite her better instincts. The rendezvous was close to her apartment, and she had been asked to wait in her car. It was a secluded spot, near a park which was deserted at that hour. Dusk had set in, and none of the street lights in the narrow lane appeared to be working.

There were a few passers-by, but no one seemed to be interested in her. Sharon glanced at her watch. It was already past the time stated by the woman. She looked around and in the rear-view mirror, feeling anxious. *Perhaps it was just some hoax.*

Suddenly, there was a sharp knock on the passenger window. Sharon could only make out the dark silhouette of a woman whose head was covered by a black scarf. She reached out and opened the door.

'Tell me what happened,' asked Kabir gently.

Neena Razdan wiped her eyes and said in a trembling voice, 'He... he tried to rape me.'

Her pink tee was stained with blood and ripped down the front, but she didn't bother to cover herself. There was a red weal on one arm as if someone had grabbed her hard there. Her hair was in disarray, and black streaks of eyeliner ran down her cheeks. She looked quite the identikit of an assault victim.

Neena had first called Kabir, crying inconsolably. She had kept the card he left behind during his visit and figured that she might as well tell him firsthand about what just happened. He would anyway get involved soon enough, given her link to Dev's case.

Kabir couldn't initially make out what she was saying but realised that something was very wrong. When she finally managed to convey that there was a dead man in her apartment, he immediately jumped on his motorcycle and sped towards Ocean West, calling SI Patil on the way.

What the hell is going on in this building? he wondered as the Bullet roared up the curving driveway.

Patil and his constables had beaten him to it by a whisker. The building manager and a neighbour were already there. Irfan lay spreadeagled on the floor in the dining room. His eyes were open wide and his mouth was agape in the rictus of violent death. A bloodied knife was next to him.

As the police team began to examine the dead body and the crime scene, Kabir ushered Neena to the drawing room and sat her down.

She continued, 'He… was Kashmiri, like me. Just a boy… barely out of his teens. Once or twice, I've… given him a cup of kahwa… our tea, you know. I never imagined that… he would try to take advantage… of my friendliness like this.'

'I saw two cups on the table. Did you offer him tea today?'

'Y-yes. He had come up… after his shift got over, looking very worried. Someone from his village was threatening him. I think that he was mixed up… with terrorists. That's why he fled from there and came to Mumbai.'

Kabir looked thoughtful. 'He told you all that today?'

Neena nodded.

'I find it strange that he would confide in you about something like that. What if you reported him to the police?'

'That's what I told him. He said that the police couldn't catch him in Kashmir and… they wouldn't be able to catch him here.'

'How exactly did he expect you to help him?'

'He… wanted money. I guess… to pay off someone.' Neena paused. 'I refused to give him anything.'

'What happened then?'

She pursed her lips. 'He began to look at me… in a strange way. I felt uncomfortable… told him that he should leave. I got up and… he grabbed me from behind.'

It struck Kabir that he should have gotten along a female officer with him, but he let her continue.

'I've… never been so scared. I screamed… and he put his hand over my mouth. He was very strong. I… tried to get out of his grip but it… was impossible. We wrestled like that for a few moments…'

She went quiet and hung her head.

Kabir said softly, 'Take your time.'

She looked up, fresh tears in her eyes. 'I suddenly saw the kitchen knife on the dining table… and managed to pick it up. He didn't notice. I let him… turn me around. He… had this crazy look in his eyes. And then…'

'You stabbed him.'

'Yes, I did.' Neena caught Kabir's hand tightly. 'Tell me… what else could I have done? He was… going to…'

'I know.'

'There was so much blood… It was awful.'

'How many times did you stab him?'

'I… don't remember. Maybe twice… thrice. I just knew that I had to…'

'Kill him?'

'No… I mean…'

Kabir interrupted. 'Why was the knife kept on the table? I guess it must be in the kitchen normally.'

'I... had cut some fruit with it... and must have forgotten to keep it back.'

'Lucky for you.'

'I don't think I've even hit anyone ever before... and now, I've just taken a life.' She shook her head.

'Did he die immediately?'

'Can't say. When he fell to the ground, I... ran into my bedroom, and locked the door.'

'I'm curious,' asked Kabir. 'Why did you call me?'

Neena thought for a moment. 'Well, we met that day... And I didn't have the number of the local thana.'

'You know you can dial 100 for the police helpline, right?'

'I guess so... My mind wasn't working. I saw your card lying on the dresser... and just called.'

'Is there anything else you want to tell me?'

She stared at him. 'Will I go to jail, DCP Kabir?'

'Difficult to say right now. It certainly looks like you've committed the act in self-defence. But all the same, a man's been killed.'

'I... I wish all this hadn't happened.'

'Where's your husband?'

'He's in Delhi on work... But he's rushing back as soon as he can.'

'We'll need to speak to him tomorrow.' Kabir stood up. 'SI Patil's team will take your statement, and the police doctor will arrive shortly. Please cooperate. It will help to close this quickly.'

23

MINNIE watched the breakers crashing on the rocks and rolling back again and again. She stood on a patch of black sand and a particularly large wave washed over her bare feet, nearly knocking her over. The sea was unusually rough, almost monsoon-like, as if it was hungry for another human life.

The spot was supposed to be closed off to the public, and the municipal corporation had even put up an iron gate at the end of the small lane that led to it. The lock on the gate had long been broken though, so Minnie had simply pushed it open and walked the few steps to the waterline.

She went there every year on that date. It was the same spot where Khuki was found, exactly eleven years ago, her frail body white and lifeless. The roiling waters had gulped her and then spat her back out. Not for the first time Minnie wondered, *could it have been an accident?* But she knew it wasn't.

Minnie remembered that fateful afternoon. She was at an event and during a break, she saw that there were several missed calls from an unknown number on her mobile. She was used to cranks doing that, but something made her call back.

'Hello, who is this?'

'Inspector Hegde with Mumbai Police, madam. We've been trying to reach you.' He paused. 'I'm afraid your sister is dead.'

Minnie's head spun. 'What… do you mean… dead?'

'I'm very sorry, madam. We found her body near the beach. She… drowned.'

The phone fell from her nerveless fingers.

A municipal worker had discovered Khuki's body that morning and informed the police. It was estimated that she hadn't been in the water for long, though it wasn't immediately clear what had happened. Unlike Minnie, Khuki couldn't swim and would never venture to wade even in calm, shallow water so it was a real mystery how she ended up in the Arabian Sea.

Khuki was studying at a reputed college in south Mumbai and living in a nearby girls' hostel at the time. Minnie wanted her to stay at her apartment in the suburbs, but it was too long a daily commute. Khuki invariably spent the weekends there though, and Minnie never failed to call her at least once every day.

She had spoken to her the previous day, but Khuki hung up after a few minutes, saying she was busy working on a project. Minnie hadn't thought anything of it, but in hindsight, she realised that there was something strange in her sister's voice. It was the last time they would ever speak to each other. *If only I had figured out that something was wrong, then maybe this wouldn't have happened,* Minnie thought bitterly.

It soon became apparent that Khuki most likely took her own life. The police found out that she had left her hostel early in the morning and jumped into a taxi. They traced the taxi driver, who said that Khuki first asked him to just drive on without specifying any destination. She was upset and crying copiously. They drove on to Bandra, where Khuki abruptly asked the driver to stop. She didn't get off but just sat in the taxi for fifteen or twenty minutes, staring blankly out of the window. Then she told him exactly where to go, and got dropped off very close to where her body was discovered.

The police questioned her friends in college and at the hostel, and it emerged that she was having a relationship with a much older man, but no one knew who he was. Minnie was shocked, and couldn't get herself to believe it. *How could Khuki hide it from me?* She'd thought again and again. It wasn't as if she never had a boyfriend earlier. They always confided everything to each other. And yet, Khuki never mentioned a word about this to Minnie.

Surprisingly, nothing in her call records revealed the identity of the mystery man. She seemed to have never spoken to him on her mobile phone. The world was only just beginning to get introduced to social media so there were no online messages, posts or photos that could provide any further clues. One of Khuki's friends had a theory that it was a professor at their college, but without a specific name, nothing could be proved. The police waited to see if anyone would own up to the relationship, but no one did, probably for fear of getting implicated in Khuki's death.

The police were keen to close the case quickly, but Minnie used all her influence to insist on a more in-depth investigation. She refused to accept that Khuki, a person who had embodied optimism and happiness, could have taken her own life. *After all, was it not possible that her secret lover had murdered her? Maybe he was married and wanted to get her out of the way. Bastard,* she thought.

It turned out to be a dead end. There was no evidence of foul play. The post-mortem showed no external injuries or anything toxic in the blood tests. It was death by drowning, plain and simple. Whether Khuki had walked into the sea on her own or got caught by a wave accidentally, was anybody's guess. Given the taxi driver's testimony, the police were inclined to believe the former and finally ruled it a suicide.

Minnie looked around. The beach further south looked remarkably clean. It used to be Mumbai's dirtiest beach until a group of environment-conscious residents of the upmarket suburb took it upon themselves to clean it up, forming a well-publicised movement that was eventually joined by thousands of people. The place where Minnie stood had changed little, though. It remained desolate and foreboding, warning people not to venture close.

If only Khuki had heeded that warning, Minnie thought, her heart aching.

Khuki. Her baby sister. The apple of her eye. More precious than her own life. The only family she still had. Sweet, cheerful, mischievous Khuki. Her smile could light up the darkest of rooms. She was a real chatterbox, always talking nineteen to the dozen in her lilting voice. Her hazel eyes, the only resemblance she had with Minnie, betrayed her every emotion. The two sisters were like chalk and cheese but incredibly close. Minnie had felt responsible for Khuki, who was seven years younger, and looked out for her as their mother would have.

She could never forgive herself for Khuki's death. She had played back their last few conversations in her mind countless times, trying to remember any signs of the turmoil that must have been raging inside Khuki. Except for that last day, she couldn't recall anything that seemed amiss. Khuki had kept up an air of normalcy remarkably well.

It was true that Minnie herself had been incredibly busy. *Maybe the signs were there. I just missed them.*

The biggest conundrum for her was why Khuki didn't tell her about this man, even if he was someone she would thoroughly disapprove of. They kept no secrets from each other. The only reason Minnie could think of was that he had somehow convinced her not to, either through threats or something else. So much so that absolutely no one could ever discover his identity, even after all these years.

Minnie felt that familiar rage rising up inside her. Khuki was just twenty, and he had preyed on her impressionable mind and eager body. It was a grave crime in Minnie's book, even if not legally so since Khuki was over the age of consent. She often wished that she could have somehow figured out who the damned man was, and punished him herself.

Justice needs to be served to all men who betrayed their women. It was unfortunate that our father was one of them.

After getting over the initial trauma, Minnie went and met each of Khuki's friends, both at her college and hostel. She knew some of them already and had heard about the others. At least, there had been no secrets there. All of them were shocked by Khuki's suicide and had no clue or warning that it was coming. In fact, everyone swore that she seemed perfectly normal in the days leading up to her death.

The theory of the boyfriend being a professor at her college seemed the most plausible one. It would explain the secrecy, as well as the fact that Khuki never needed to call him from her mobile. Minnie obtained a roster of the male staff at the college and dug into their backgrounds as much as she could. But the list was long, and it was impossible to pin down anyone. The police could have done it if they wished, but they refused to launch a witch-hunt at a well-known educational institution without any concrete evidence to begin with. As far as they were concerned, no crime had been committed anyway.

Minnie was finally forced to give up, broken with grief and helplessness. The only thing she could hope for was that Khuki had done everything of her own free will and that there had been no coercion of any kind. After all, there were so many horror stories of predatory men forcing young girls into sexual relationships through blackmail, threats, or false promises.

Khuki's post-mortem had revealed a disturbing but not entirely unexpected fact. *She was pregnant.* Minnie knew that was probably what drove Khuki over the edge. She had been a conservative and moralistic person, and finding herself in such a situation would have been devastating.

If only she had told me, especially after learning about her pregnancy.

It was very difficult for Minnie to accept that her sister could have killed herself, whatever the provocation. She had never gotten over her suspicion that Khuki could have been murdered. Maybe she had come there that day for a tryst with her lover and he had pushed her into the sea, knowing very well that she couldn't swim. It didn't matter whether it was premeditated or in the heat of the moment.

Minnie sighed and began to walk back from the beach, her face moist with tears. Time hadn't diminished the crushing sadness or her burning desire to avenge Khuki, but that day, she felt a strange sense of calm, a sudden feeling that Khuki was at peace, wherever she was.

A debt had been paid, even if indirectly.

24

'I didn't know you were so brave, Harish.' Kabir winked at him.

Patil looked up, his mouth full of meen porichathu, a spicy fried rawas, and a dreamy expression on his face. The two of them were sitting at Rice Boat, a restaurant just off the Western Highway specialising in Kerala cuisine. After the formalities at Neena Razdan's apartment were completed, Patil insisted on taking Kabir for dinner.

'It's my treat, sir. To hell with my diet.' 'It's only one meal. She'll never know, sir.'

Kabir grinned. 'That's if I don't tell her.'

There was a pleading look in Patil's eyes.

The waiter arrived with plates of konju olathiathu, braised prawns with coconut slivers, and kanai kozhi, chicken fried with green spices. For a few minutes, both men dug into the food, washing it down with gulps of Kingfisher draught.

Kabir wiped his mouth and said, 'I don't believe that woman.'

'Neena Razdan?'

'Yes, Harish. Her story doesn't ring true.'

'Why do you say so, sir?'

'First of all, she seemed quite calm for someone who had just killed her would-be rapist.'

'But she was upset, crying…'

Kabir interrupted. 'Yes Harish, but if things had happened as she told us, she should have been *traumatised.* Being almost raped and then killing a man would have sent any normal person into a state of absolute shock. You and I have seen many victims of such situations…'

'The crime scene corroborated her statement, sir.'

'Wasn't it too convenient that the kitchen knife happened to be right there on the dining table?'

'She said she had cut fruit with it earlier.'

Kabir leaned forward. 'I checked the kitchen and the garbage bin. There were no fruit peels, seeds… nothing. It's unlikely she would have eaten everything. Then why use the knife at all?'

Patil was silent.

Kabir took a bite of aatirachi, a minced mutton cutlet, and said, 'The boy Irfan looked strong. It wouldn't have been easy for Mrs Razdan to have broken his hold and attack him back.'

'So what do you think really happened?'

'I don't know yet. But I think there was something else between her and that boy.'

'You mean they could have been in a consensual sexual relationship, sir?'

'It's certainly possible.' Kabir pondered aloud. 'We already know that she's not faithful to her husband. And older women fancy young men, do they not?'

'Do they?' Patil looked wistful. 'No such luck for me when I was young, sir.'

Kabir laughed. 'You needed to be in the right place at the right time, Harish.'

'Seeing how it ended for this boy, I should be having no regrets.' Patil grimaced.

'I found it very odd that he would be confiding in her about his past misdeeds. We still live in a very feudal country, Harish. The socio-economic and cultural gap between the security guard and a flat-owner in a building, especially one as luxurious as this one, is enormous.'

'I guess they bonded over their common Kashmiri roots.'

Kabir shook his head. 'No Harish, I'm convinced it can't be that alone. There has to be more.'

'We'll do another round of questioning at Ocean West tomorrow. If there's something else, I'm sure it will come out.'

'Has the boy's family been informed?'

'The security agency has the name of his village but no contact details.'

'Send a message to the village thana as soon as possible.'

Before Patil could respond, his phone rang. He picked up and said gruffly, 'Yes, Shinde. What is it?'

After a few minutes, he hung up and exclaimed, 'You were perfectly right, sir!'

'What did he say?'

'Irfan's phone was dead when we found it at the scene. They've now charged it and guess what?'

Kabir waited to hear more.

'It seems that he had quietly recorded the final conversation between Neena Razdan and himself. Everything's on tape.'

'It'll be better for you if you tell us everything.' Kabir's tone was low but menacing.

Neena Razdan sat on a rickety chair in an interrogation room at the Crime Branch headquarters, her head bowed. A female constable stood impassively behind her, while Kabir paced about like an angry tiger. Patil sat across the rusted metal table, holding up Irfan's phone.

They had brought in Neena at seven o'clock in the morning. According to a Supreme Court ruling, a woman can't be arrested between sundown and sunrise. In case she was accused of a serious crime, the police had to get written permission from a magistrate before they could arrest her in the middle of the night. Since there was no time for that, Patil had posted a team outside Neena's apartment to make sure she didn't abscond and waited until daybreak.

Neena had protested vehemently, and the two stout female constables had to practically drag her out of her place. She shouted threats and abuse until Patil told her about the recording made by Irfan. It deflated her in an instant, and she came along quietly after that, seemingly resigned to her fate.

'Well?' Kabir leaned over the table, his face close to hers.

Neena looked up, her eyes teary and bloodshot. 'I want my lawyer here.'

Kabir glanced at Patil, and then back at her. 'You certainly have the right to a lawyer. But please understand, we'll get to the truth anyway. This is a murder case. If you try to hide anything, it'll be much worse for you.'

Neena thought furiously. Patil had only played back the beginning of the recording on Irfan's phone. She hadn't credited the boy with so much cunning. *Sneaky bastard. He had come prepared to get me on tape, and then blackmail me. Good thing I killed him,* she fumed inwardly. But now that the police had it, she was in big trouble.

Neena tried to remember what she had said to Irfan. He had placed the phone on the dining table and they had sat there right through so it would have picked up the entire conversation. She knew she had said things to seduce him at the end so that evidence would be damning for her, but maybe there was still a way out, if she played her cards well.

She took a deep breath. 'Listen, DCP Kabir, you've got this totally wrong.'

'Have I?'

'Whatever you heard me say on the recording, it's… it's not what it sounds like. As I told you before, I was getting very uncomfortable with the way Irfan was looking at me. I realised that… I had put myself in a dangerous situation.'

She paused, then said, 'Can I please… have some water?'

Patil nodded to the constable, who went out and fetched a small Bisleri bottle.

Neena took a long pull of the water and continued, 'It struck me then that I had to distract him somehow and protect myself. The boy was very strong. If he attacked me, I… I wouldn't be able to fight back so I decided to act like… I was seducing him. The knife was on the table, within my reach…'

Kabir interrupted loudly. 'That's a likely story! Do you really expect us to believe you?'

'Sir, let Madam continue. Please.' Patil's voice was almost pleasant. He and Kabir had automatically switched to the time-tested good-cop-bad-cop mode.

Neena went on, 'I… As I was saying, I let him… touch me… and then, he…' She stopped.

'Yes?'

'You… know what happened after that.'

Patil smiled at her. 'Why was the knife on the table? You had told us that you cut fruit with it, but we found nothing in the kitchen.'

She looked away. 'I… don't remember. Maybe it was already there… from earlier.'

Kabir sneered. 'Yes, very convenient, wasn't it?'

'Why the hell should I make all this up?' Neena glared at him. 'I called you for help and… now I'm the accused. Is this how the police treat victims?'

'Let's not forget that you killed a man violently less than twelve hours ago.'

'It was in self-defence!' Neena exclaimed. 'You're men. You won't understand.'

Kabir's eyes blazed. 'Oh, I understand perfectly well the game you're trying to play here.'

She folded her arms. 'I refuse to say anything more until my lawyer arrives.'

There was silence for a few seconds.

Both men knew that they were treading on dangerous ground. There was a thin line between trying to get a confession and intimidating the suspect. Not that it would have mattered otherwise, for the police routinely did much worse during interrogation. But here they were dealing with a spirited woman who came from an affluent background and was apparently a victim of attempted sexual assault herself. If there was one thing to be worried about these days, it was bad publicity.

'Okay, madam. Let us assume that you killed Irfan because he was going to rape you,' said Patil finally. 'But the question remains. Why didn't you just run out of the apartment if you felt so scared? What was the need to kill the boy in the manner you did?'

'You simply have no idea how a woman feels in such a situation, do you? And besides, a rapist deserves nothing less than death!'

Patil nodded imperceptibly to Kabir and picked up Irfan's phone again. 'All that now remains to ask you is about the first part of your conversation with Irfan.'

Kabir came around and stood next to Neena. His voice rose in a crescendo. 'Whom did you pay Irfan to murder?'

She blanched but stared back defiantly at him. 'I'm not saying another word.'

25

WHEN Tanya heard about what had happened with Neena Razdan, she felt no sympathy. *That slut deserved it. And why the hell did Dev have to be the way he was?* she thought. She knew all about their affair, of course.

She sighed. It had been wonderful with Dev while it lasted.

When they started seeing each other, Tanya's career was really taking off. She was already a household name in the television industry and had landed a leading role in a prominent film, a whodunit based on a classic detective series, for which she had to travel for a month-long shoot in Darjeeling.

To Tanya's delight, she saw Dev sitting two rows behind her on the aircraft. He had decided to surprise her, managing to get the last seat on the flight to Bagdogra. The film crew had booked up the Mayfair Hotel, but Tanya was staying at the Darjeeling Planters Club, a place that reminded her of her childhood. She insisted that Dev take a room at the club, though he had made a reservation at another hotel.

The next morning, they sat on cane chairs on the long veranda, sipping flavourful tea in porcelain cups and eating delicious omelettes whipped up by a chef who appeared to be as ancient as the establishment itself. It was a clear day, and they enjoyed a breathtaking view of the mighty Kanchenjunga in all its snowy glory. Tanya soon left for her shoot, rather reluctantly, while Dev spent the rest of the day exploring the charming hill station.

The next four weeks were idyllic. Dev began to accompany Tanya to her shoots, often getting mistaken as the hero of the film, much to the irritation of the real leading man. They would go for long walks in the mornings, and curl up by the fireplace in the evenings with mugs of hot chocolate. There was a break in the schedule due to some technical issue, and the two of them went off to spend the time at a luxurious tea estate in Kurseong.

At the end of it, Dev and Tanya were completely in love with each other. On the way back, they spent a day in Kolkata due to a last-minute flight cancellation. On an impulse, they went and got married at the famous Kalighat Temple.

To Dev's credit, he remained faithful to Tanya for over a year. It was the longest he had ever been committed to one woman.

He did love her, with more fervour than he had felt for anyone else before. It felt nice to have someone in his bed as a companion, not just a lover. Tanya worked long, erratic hours and he often cooked for her, reviving an old talent. She renovated his bachelor pad, bringing in the warmth and colour that the apartment had sorely lacked. They went for impromptu coffee dates, binge-watched television, bought surprise gifts for each other, and argued about where to build a holiday home. It was all very romantic.

However, as they say, a leopard doesn't change its spots. On a flight to Bengaluru, where he was travelling to speak at a conference, Dev found himself sitting next to a woman in her late forties, who turned out to be the CEO of a well-known multinational company. She was also invited to speak at the same event.

It was clear that she was interested in him, and Dev found her attractive in a severe, no-nonsense kind of way. She had the body of a woman fifteen years younger but had kept the grey in her hair, which he found sexy. Nevertheless, he was surprised when there was a knock on his door soon after they had checked in at the hotel, and he opened it to find her standing there in a short dress, holding a bottle of wine and two glasses. Dev hesitated, but years of habit made him step aside and let her walk in.

He felt guilty later and thought about confessing to Tanya. Better sense prevailed, but the floodgates had been opened. Dev went back to his old ways, albeit discreetly. He told himself that he still loved Tanya and any little flings on the side were never serious, nothing more than physical encounters, including with Neena Razdan.

Until he met Sharon Sequeira.

'Sir, do you think Neena Razdan paid the boy, Irfan, to murder Dev Malik?'

Kabir didn't respond to Patil immediately. After the first interrogation ended with Neena refusing to talk further, they retired to his office to discuss what to do next. He swivelled in his chair and looked outside. There had been an unseasonal shower the previous night, and the winter pollution was temporarily washed away. The leaves of the peepal tree visible through one corner of the window glistened in the morning sun.

Kabir finally turned around and picked up a vada pav from the paper plate kept on his desk. He said, 'It's possible, very possible. That woman was obsessed with him.'

He pointed to the plate and nodded questioningly. Patil looked longingly at the one remaining vada pav for a couple of moments, then shook his head.

Kabir suppressed a smile. 'Harish, did you check if Irfan was in Ocean West when Dev was murdered?'

'He had gone off duty by eight that night and was relieved by the night guard who later raised the alarm and discovered the body. Interestingly, Irfan didn't sign out in the register kept at the main gate that night. The security supervisor told us that it was against the rules, but it did happen once in a while, especially when the building staff exited by a side gate that was supposed to be kept closed but often wasn't.'

Kabir looked thoughtful. 'So, it's likely that Irfan remained inside the premises after his shift was over.'

'Yes, sir. He was last seen exiting the lobby at 8.10 p.m. No one remembers seeing him after that, nor does he appear in any of the CCTV footage from that night.'

'Irfan knew his way around the place and was obviously a cunning fellow. If he wanted to get up to Dev's apartment without being spotted, I guess he would have found a way.'

'Very simple, sir!' Patil exclaimed. 'He could have walked down to the basement, and taken the lift from there. There's no CCTV coverage there, and also remember that the cameras inside two of the lifts weren't working.'

Kabir leaned forward. 'After I first spoke to Neena Razdan, I was speculating that she herself could have gone up to Dev's apartment that night without being seen. She lives in the same tower, after all. Now it appears that it could just as well have been Irfan.'

'Exactly. She must have paid him well to do the job. From what we've gathered about the boy, he was bad news.'

'Did you hear back from Kashmir about him?'

'Yes, it seems Irfan was linked to a terrorist group there. He fled to Mumbai when the police were closing in on him.'

'So he wasn't new to crime, and Neena Razdan must have known that.' Kabir paused. 'One thing is that there was no sign of a struggle in Dev's apartment. He was a strongly built man, and it wouldn't have been easy for Irfan to overpower him.'

Patil pursed his lips. 'You're right about that, sir. Nevertheless, everything else fits the theory, no?'

He continued, 'In the phone recording, Irfan refers to some other man who wasn't supposed to be there, and then Neena replies that it's been "taken care of".' Patil's eyes gleamed. 'I believe they could have been talking about Harry Shah, sir! We know from the handprint that he had gone to Dev's place that evening.'

'Hmm... So you think they murdered Harry as well, maybe because he saw something?'

'That's right, sir.'

Kabir got up and stretched his arms. He sensed that the investigation was nearing conclusion, though he couldn't bring himself to accept yet that they had cracked it.

He came around and sat on the edge of his desk. 'We mustn't forget about Sharon Sequeira, Harish.'

'Sir, there's a half-hour gap between her departure and the discovery of Dev's body. That's enough time for Irfan to have gone in and committed the crime.'

'So if she's innocent, why did she disappear?'

'Maybe Irfan killed her too?'

Kabir looked unconvinced. 'That doesn't sound right, Harish. Sharon Sequeira is involved in this somehow, I'm sure of that.'

Patil persisted. 'Sir, we know that Neena Razdan was very jealous of her. She told you so herself. What if she knew that Ms Sequeira was going for dinner at Dev's place that night, and planned everything so that suspicion would fall on her?'

'Then it's a perfect murder.'

26

KABIR stared at the serene waters of the Arabian Sea, sipping on the strawberry milkshake he had picked up from Bachelor's. The eighty-year-old Charni Road eatery was wildly popular, but he always thought it to be overrated, with only the shakes worth their steep prices.

Needing to clear his head, Kabir jumped on his Bullet and headed for Girgaum Chowpatty, one of his favourite spots in the city. As a child, his father would take him there every Sunday evening for a bowl of bhel and the incomparable ice gola. He loved the buzz of the crowded beach and the soothing sound of the breaking waves.

It was quite deserted at that time of the day though, which suited Kabir just fine. He needed to think calmly. The Dev Malik case had become an albatross around his neck, threatening his career. Even the commissioner had stopped calling him, assuming that the investigation wasn't going anywhere.

It was true that Patil's theory of Neena and Irfan conspiring to murder Dev Malik was a compelling one, but they needed proof. The boy was dead, and the woman was unlikely to confess. They had no evidence to conclusively place either of them at Dev's apartment that night. If Harry Shah had been silenced later by the same duo, there was nothing to pin them to his death either.

And then there was Sharon Sequeira. *Where the hell was she?* Since she hadn't been traced for so many days, it was quite likely that she was dead. Maybe Patil was correct. *Neena Razdan could have had Irfan kill her as well.* Kabir had to admit that it was a perfect set-up. And yet, he still found it difficult to credit her with so much cunning. When he had met Neena the first time, she had seemed neurotic and unstable, not a cold and calculating murderer.

Kabir's reverie was broken by a sharp tap on his leg. He saw that it was a boy, no more than seven or eight years old.

The boy looked up at him and said, 'Can you please move your motorcycle?'

Kabir smiled. 'Now, why should I do that?'

'I want to play here.'

'But the whole beach is empty. Why don't you play anywhere else?'

The boy crossed his arms. 'I like to play only here.'

Kabir shrugged. 'I don't see anything special about this place.'

'It's special, don't you know? The sand is deep and it's not close to the water. And my father can see me while I'm here.'

On cue, a man came running up and caught the boy's hand. 'Enough! Come along now.'

Kabir asked, 'Are you this boy's father?'

The man looked at him with trepidation. He had figured out that Kabir was a policeman. He said nervously, 'Yes, I am. I'm sorry he bothered you, sir.'

'What do you do?'

'I... I'm a balloon seller, sir.'

Kabir smiled again. He remembered that the Sunday evening outing to Chowpatty would always end with his father buying a colourful balloon for him. He thought of his own daughter, *I wonder why I've never got her here.* The answer was obvious, of course. Children have so many distractions and occupations nowadays. Going to a beach meant a holiday in Goa, at the very least.

He sighed. The man began to walk away, pulling the reluctant boy. Suddenly, something caught Kabir's eye and he called out, 'Wait!'

They stopped.

Kabir stared at the paper cone in the man's other hand. It contained roasted peanuts, but that's not what interested him. The three-letter name of the newspaper from which the cone had been made was clearly visible. Kabir slapped his forehead, for it reminded him that he needed to follow up on something crucial. *DNA.*

He got up on the Bullet and started the engine. 'I'm leaving anyway. Let him play here.'

The boy grinned.

Kabir took out a five-hundred-rupee note and handed it to his father. 'Spend it on a nice meal.'

He wheeled around in a cloud of sand and sped away.

As Kabir returned to his office, he found Nusrat standing outside his door.

'Ah Nusrat, just the person I wanted to see. Come on in.'

'I was waiting for you, sir,' she said and followed him inside.

Kabir got a whiff of her perfume and looked behind, despite himself. Nusrat was looking exceptionally attractive, he thought. She normally didn't put on any make-up but had lined her eyes and even dabbed some lipstick that day. And instead of the usual jeans, she was wearing a navy blue skirt that ended just above her knees, paired with a cream blouse of some expensive material.

He couldn't help saying, 'You're looking… nice, Nusrat. Any special occasion today?'

She smiled. 'It's my birthday.'

'Oh, many happy returns of the day then.' He felt vaguely embarrassed that he hadn't known.

'Thank you, sir.'

Kabir flopped down in his chair and motioned her to sit across his desk. 'So, what is it that you wanted to tell me, Nusrat?'

She bit back her disappointment that he had moved on to business so quickly, and said, 'Well, I had a look at Harry Shah's call records, like you asked me to. The last call on his phone, early on the morning of his death, is from a ghost prepaid number. It's in the name of an eighty-three-year-old woman from Virar who obviously isn't the actual user of that connection.'

Kabir didn't respond. He wondered if the mystery caller was none other than Neena Razdan.

Nusrat continued, 'In fact, there are several calls to Harry's phone from that number, with the first one on the day after Dev's death, sir.'

'So this person gets in touch with Harry and eventually calls him to the rendezvous at Aarey, then kills him. The question is why.'

'Maybe Harry saw something at Dev's apartment that night? We know he was there, sir.'

'Why didn't he report it to us?'

'He was a shady character, wasn't he? I'm sure the last thing he would want to do is go to the police for anything.'

'Hmm… You could be right, Nusrat.'

'I wonder if this person was blackmailing Harry in some way, sir? He had enough secrets, I'm sure.'

'That's possible, but it would have to be somehow connected to Dev. The timing is too much of a coincidence.'

'Maybe they *were* in a relationship?' Nusrat giggled. 'Dev was quite irresistible, sir.'

Kabir snorted.

Nusrat changed the topic. 'By the way, why did you want to see me in the first place?'

'Ah yes. Did we get the DNA results of the hair found on Harry Shah's corpse?'

'The FSL called yesterday to say that they've completed the analysis. We compared it against our DNA databank but found no matches. Not that I was expecting anything. You know how it is, sir.'

'The pathologist who did the autopsy had told me that the hair probably belonged to a woman. Is that the case?'

'The DNA is female, that much is certain.'

'I need you to do something, Nusrat. We have to check if the hair belongs to Neena Razdan.'

'Neena Razdan, sir?'

'Oh, you're not updated about the events from last night. Patil will brief you. His team should be able to provide something from her effects that can be used for obtaining a DNA sample. Tell forensics that I want the analysis done in twenty-four hours.'

'I'll get on it right away.' She saluted and walked out.

A few minutes later, something else struck Kabir and he called Nusrat back in. Her eyes widened as she listened to his additional instructions.

When Dev opened the door that evening, he was surprised to see Harry Shah standing there.

'You?' he exclaimed.

'Can I please come in?'

Dev frowned. 'What do you want?' But he stepped aside and allowed Harry to come into the foyer.

Harry said hesitantly, 'I... just came to apologise.'

Dev remained silent.

'That evening... I was really stupid. I don't know... what I was thinking.'

'Yes, it was incredibly stupid.'

Harry rubbed his jaw and grimaced. 'You did give me a lesson for it, which I won't forget in a hurry.'

Dev said indignantly, 'You're very lucky I didn't report you to the police.'

'I know.' Harry folded his hands. 'I'm grateful you didn't.'

'So why are you really here?' Dev knew enough about Harry to be sure that there was something else he had come for.

He was right.

Harry was in a deep financial hole. Yet again. He had become persona non grata in most of his erstwhile networks, and this time, even his father had sworn not to bail him out. Law enforcement agencies were closing in on him as a suspect in economic crimes, instead of just a person of interest. A lifetime of misdeeds was about to catch up with Harry, and for a change, he could see no way out.

Until one evening at his regular nightclub, Harry struck up a conversation with a young entrepreneur, who happened to be the founder of an e-commerce start-up specialising in luxury goods. The twenty-something-year-old spoke about the burgeoning market of high-net-worth individuals in India, especially in the tier-II cities, and how all of them wanted to own a Louis Vuitton bag, or Ferragamo shoes, or an Armani suit. He had set up an online marketplace for buyers and sellers but was facing a major issue of fakes, which threatened his entire venture.

Harry listened impassively, smelling an opportunity. The next morning, as they lay in bed after an energetic night, he began to speak about his own early years in the luxury business, without mentioning that he used to deal in the very same fakes that his companion was complaining about. Rather, he suggested with a practised air of confidence that he had extensive knowledge of the trade and the target segment, including how to spot and weed out fakes.

The young man sat up and listened with interest, immediately realising that Harry knew what he was talking about. By the time they finished breakfast, he said the words with the brash impulsiveness Harry had been counting on: 'Will you work with me?'

Harry pretended to be surprised, then thought about it and finally said, 'Why not?'

It was true that he could bring his unique experience to genuinely help his new lover. A thief to catch a thief. A nice job in a well-funded start-up could ease his financial woes quickly, and the customary stake in the company could well turn lucrative in the not-too-distant future.

There was a problem, though. The investors had to be informed. And one of them was Dev Malik.

'Look, Dev,' Harry began. 'I know we've started out on the wrong foot, but I'm sure we can put the past behind us.'

'Well… All right.'

'Uh… Maybe I can work for you in some way. I believe you're an active investor in a number of companies?'

'Yes, but I rarely get involved in any operational matters.'

'I met this young man recently, who…'

Dev interrupted. 'Listen, I'm expecting someone just now. Can we talk about this another time?'

After a moment's hesitation, Harry said, 'All right. I'll come back later.'

As he walked towards the staircase, the lift doors dinged open, and he stopped. A tall woman in a red dress stepped out. Harry had never seen her before but thought she looked vaguely familiar.

He smiled at her, but she ignored him.

When the woman passed Harry, something made him turn around. He watched her ring the doorbell outside Dev's apartment, a puzzled expression on his face.

27

The old man was awake and reading his Kindle in bed, when he heard a car braking across the road. He immediately knew who it was. The fluorescent clock on the side table showed that it was exactly 10.30 p.m. He got up, threw a shawl around himself and looked out through the tall window of his gazebo.

There was the by-now familiar white car waiting outside the yellow villa, as the automated gate slid open slowly with a faint hum. He was surprised to see that the car's lights were off. As he watched on, the gate stopped halfway, making a harsh, grating noise as if one of its gears had slipped.

The sound of a muffled curse wafted up to the man in the cold, still air. The driver's door of the car opened, and a tall figure stepped out. He knew that it had to be her, even though it was dark and she was wearing a hoodie. She bent down, presumably to switch off the motor, and then pushed open the gate herself.

She got back into the car and drove in. Unusually, she parked behind the villa, outside his line of vision. He wondered if she knew he was watching. She walked around to the front door and looked up, seemingly straight in his direction, before disappearing inside the house. Even though he was standing in complete darkness, for there was a power cut, the man shrank back involuntarily.

She must have seen me.

He shivered suddenly, and not from the cold. He wondered why. There was no reason to be scared. After all, he knew his neighbour. She was definitely no criminal. In fact, her profession touched so many lives in a good way. And yet, her recent visits had been strange, to say the least. She came and went at odd hours, and was barely to be seen outdoors. *That rather defeated the purpose of having a home in such a beautiful place, didn't it?*

As the man returned to bed, a nagging thought came back to him: *What if it's not her?*

She could certainly have allowed someone else to use her house, but in that case, that person was up to something dubious. It definitely wasn't normal behaviour for someone enjoying a vacation home. He wondered if he should give her a call to check, but he didn't have her number.

The man was an avid reader of pulp fiction and couldn't help letting his imagination run wild with conspiracy theories. *What if something nefarious was going on inside that villa?* The possibilities in his mind ranged from drugs to prostitution and even murder.

He wondered if he should call the police anyway, then dismissed the thought. If it turned out to be a false alarm, he would look like a fool. As he drifted off to sleep, his last thought was that it wasn't really any of his business.

The car drove out a couple of hours later. The power was still gone, but she didn't switch on the headlights until she had exited the community gate and left the familiar signboard well behind. Instead of the Expressway, she took the old highway and headed towards Pune, going dangerously fast.

The final job was done, and she was convinced that it had gone perfectly. The entire sequence of events was almost incredible, like a nightmare which you could never wake up from. Things had often threatened to spin out of control, but her strong instinct of self-preservation had saved the day.

Anyway, it was now coming to an end and she was relieved.

The driver of the minibus stifled a yawn. He hadn't slept in thirty-six hours, having been on the road for most of that time. One of the other drivers had had an accident, not with any of the agency vehicles, but while riding his own scooter. So now he was forced into extended duty. He didn't mind, for the extra money was welcome and he was anyway used to pulling long hours.

He had taken a raucous corporate group up to Panchgani the previous evening. They were heading for a three-day offsite and clearly in great spirits, for the singing and laughter had continued non-stop all the way from Panvel. Until they ran into heavy traffic an hour out from their destination. A container truck had broken down on the two-lane road pretending to be a state highway, backing up vehicles on both sides in serpentine queues.

It was past ten o'clock at night when they finally reached the resort. By then, all the merriment of his passengers had faded. They were hungry and tempers were frayed. He was angry with the delay too, for it meant that he would have to drive back to Mumbai through the night, as there was another booking in the morning. After unloading the group and their luggage, he had a light dinner and set out again.

There was still an hour left for daybreak. He had crossed Lonavala and with a little luck, there would be time for a snooze before the next pick-up. Just then, there was a loud report followed by a hissing sound, and the minibus wobbled. The driver muttered a string of expletives, for he knew there had been a puncture. He stopped and saw that it was a front tyre, which meant it would have to be changed immediately.

He woke up the helper, who was snoozing on one of the empty rows of seats behind, as he cursed himself for not having taken the Expressway. It was a very dark spot. He kept the headlights on and fumbled for the jack and spare tyre. Once the tools were laid out, he sent the helper to fetch some stones to prevent the minibus from rolling. The boy went reluctantly, flashing the torch of his mobile phone from side to side.

A few moments later, he shouted, '*Anna*, come here quickly!'

The driver ran behind him. There was a wide clearing next to the road, sloping sharply down towards a large tree standing at an angle from the incline. A white car had crashed into it head-on. There was a strong smell of diesel in the air. A wisp of smoke trailed out from under the crumpled bonnet. It was clear that the accident hadn't happened too long back.

Guided by the light from the boy's phone, the driver went up to the ill-fated car and looked inside. It had only one occupant, slumped over the steering wheel in the driver's seat. As he looked carefully, he realised that it was a *woman.* Both of them tried to open the door, but it was completely jammed.

He asked the helper to fetch the lug wrench. With it, he managed to break the window glass of the rear door and force it open. They gently pulled out the unconscious woman and laid her on the grass. She had a deep gash on her forehead and was covered with blood. The driver had seen his share of accidents and knew from the force of the impact that she likely had serious internal injuries as well. Her breathing was very shallow, but she was alive, at least.

He took out his mobile phone but realised that there was no network. Instructing the boy to stay with the woman, he ran back to the road. After a few minutes, headlights appeared in the distance and he flailed his arms wildly. Normally, no one would have stopped at that time of night, but it turned out to be a truck being driven by an old sardar who had many years of experience on Indian highways. He realised instinctively that this was no robbery attempt but a genuine call for help.

The driver was relieved to see the truck slow down and stop behind his minibus. He quickly narrated the situation to the sardar, who told him that there was a police check post a few kilometres down the road. Knowing that time was of the essence, the sardar immediately agreed to take the injured woman there, and they carried her carefully to the back of the truck.

As is their wont, the two police constables at the checkpoint were extremely suspicious when the truck arrived with the unconscious woman. They assumed that either the sardar had assaulted her or hit her with his truck. He was prepared for that of course, having seen similar situations in the past. Patiently explaining to them that it was critical to get urgent medical attention for the woman, he offered to wait there until they could verify his story.

When the woman was taken to a nearby rural primary health centre, the young intern on duty took one look at her and shook his head. He said that there was nothing he could do for her with the limited facilities at his disposal, and suggested that she be driven to a hospital in Panvel, which was forty-five minutes away.

By the time the woman was admitted there and a proper doctor began to examine her, she had slipped into a coma.

28

'So you're Mrs Neena Razdan's husband?'

'Yes, I am.'

SI Patil stared at him for a moment. The man looked distinguished, with a patrician face and silver streaks in his thick, brushed-back hair. He was broad and heavily built, if slightly overweight. The jacket was clearly expensive, and the spotless white of his shirt belied the fact that he had just got off an early morning flight. There was a tall cup of Starbucks coffee in his hand.

They were at the Worli thana, seated in Patil's large but cluttered office. He leaned forward and said, 'You know what your wife has done?'

The man replied calmly, 'She called me last night. I do know she stabbed that security guard.'

'Murdered him, in fact.'

There was no response.

'Why do you think she killed him?'

'I don't know. But Neena told me that he had entered the house and was threatening her.'

'You believe her?'

'I suppose so.'

Patil sat back in his chair and folded his arms. He figured that this man was a cool customer, surprisingly unfazed by what had happened. Nor did he seem particularly keen to defend his wife. *There's clearly trouble in this marriage,* he mused.

He persisted. 'You think she may be lying?'

The man rolled his eyes. 'Well, it wouldn't be the first time.'

'Did your wife know this boy Irfan well?'

'I shouldn't think so.' He frowned. 'Though now that I recall, I'm sure I had seen the fellow a couple of weeks back when I was in town the last time.'

'In the building, I assume.'

'No, that's the thing. I was out on my usual morning walk and it was still dark. The lanes were pretty deserted. Suddenly, this guy came out of nowhere and I stopped, assuming he wanted to say something to me. He was wearing a cap but seemed familiar. I'm quite certain it was this same Irfan.'

Patil listened with interest. 'Go on.'

'Abruptly, the chap turned around and hurried away. It was very strange. I shouted after him, but he didn't look back.'

'Did he say anything to you at all?'

'No. It was like he was about to say something and then decided not to.'

'Was there anyone else around?'

'I… don't remember. As I told you earlier, it was early morning and the sun hadn't yet risen. But I was walking alone, as I always do.' He paused. 'Actually, there may have been another man walking a short distance behind me.'

There was silence for a few moments.

Then Patil asked, 'Did you feel that Irfan might have been threatening you?'

The man looked thoughtful. 'That hadn't struck me. It was certainly an odd encounter. In hindsight, it's possible. He was clearly coming up to me before something threw him off.'

'I need to tell you something, sir.' Patil rubbed his forehead. 'We have proof that your wife paid this boy Irfan to kill someone, and he was blackmailing her over that.'

The man's eyes went wide.

'Well, what do you have to say to that?'

The man shook his head. 'If that is really the case, inspector, I can tell you that the target could very likely have been *me*.'

Dawn had already broken when the police jeep rolled up to the accident spot, accompanied by a small tow truck. After the sardar took away the woman, the minibus driver had hurriedly changed the flat tyre, and driven off. He didn't want to get embroiled in any hassles with the police. The main thing was that the woman needed medical attention, which he had helped with. After that, it was none of his business.

The sub-inspector who was roused from sleep and asked to investigate the matter was in a foul mood. He couldn't understand all the fuss. The driver must have been drunk, he figured and crashed the car. It wasn't the first time he had seen that, especially with all the new bungalows being built in the hills, and the crazy parties that went on there. However, a woman was involved and there was always the possibility of a crime having been committed, so he was forced to go himself.

As he walked around, the circumstances became clear. There were prominent skid marks where the car had veered sharply off the road and gone into the clearing at high speed. The road curved at that point so either the woman hadn't seen that or she had turned to avoid an oncoming vehicle and lost control.

The sub-inspector did a cursory examination of the interior of the car. There were bloodstains on the driver's seat and dashboard. Pieces of glass from the smashed windscreen were all over the floor mats. He opened the glove compartment, and the registration papers revealed that the car belonged to a Mumbai agency. However, there was no clue to the identity of the person who had rented it.

Surprisingly, there were no personal items of the driver to be found. He would have expected at least a handbag, for in his experience, no woman travelled anywhere without one. *Maybe the truck driver stole it.* Though not apparently damaged, the trunk wouldn't open. After trying a few times, he gave up and decided to let the people at the workshop look at it later. He didn't know then that there was something inside the trunk that would turn out to be very significant.

He figured out the place where the minibus had stopped and the truck behind it. The wide tyre marks were clearly visible in the moist earth. However, there was another set of smaller tyre marks slightly ahead, indicating that another vehicle, probably a car, had also stopped there before driving on. The sub-inspector shook his head. *The sardar hadn't mentioned this third vehicle in his statement.*

As the car was pulled back from the tree, he noted that the damage seemed less than what he had initially thought. From the distance it had travelled after careening off the road, the car must have been going at a fairly high speed. And yet, the impact wasn't as devastating as he would have expected. *Maybe she managed to apply the brakes at the last minute. Yet, it was definitely strange.*

As the tow truck moved off with the wrecked car, the sub-inspector made some notes in a small diary and took several photos of the scene with his mobile phone. There wasn't any forensics unit available in a rural jurisdiction, nor did he think it was necessary since there was no evidence of any crime having been committed. Yet, it was good that the constables at the checkpoint had the sense to detain the truck driver. He would have to speak to the man himself later to clear up a few points.

The sub-inspector was thankful that it was a remote spot; hence, there were no people around. Otherwise, the presence of a police jeep would have certainly attracted a crowd of curious onlookers. A couple of vehicles driving by slowed down to see what was happening, but he waved them on irritatedly.

Back at his station later, he called the rental agency named in the ill-fated car's registration papers. In such matters, a personal visit was always more effective, but it didn't make any sense for him to go all the way to the city just for that. A message to the concerned thana could have helped, though he wasn't sure they would give his request much priority as it was just a road accident. However, it was important to identify the injured woman quickly so that her family could be informed.

The receptionist who picked up was polite but insisted that she couldn't share any information over the phone. After some angry threats from the sub-inspector, she reluctantly transferred the call to a manager, who realised that he was dealing with an annoyed policeman and that it was better to give him what he wanted. He punched the licence plate number of the car into his computer and read out the name that came up on his screen.

The name immediately rang a bell in the sub-inspector's mind, and he placed another call, this time to the Mumbai Crime Branch.

The commissioner sat with her arms folded, a grim expression on her face. Behind her was the Indian flag and the backlit emblem of the Mumbai Police. The office was enormous, with a high ceiling, a wide, gleaming desk and extensive wooden panelling. Yet, it somehow seemed spartan and uncluttered, much like the personality of its current incumbent.

Kabir had been in that office twice before, on both occasions to be commended for cracking important cases. When he was summoned this time though, he knew that no such pleasantries awaited him. It would be a difficult meeting.

As was her wont, the commissioner got straight to the point. 'I hear you finally have a suspect in the Dev Malik case in custody?'

Kabir hesitated for a moment, then said, 'We've detained a woman, a Neena Razdan, for the killing of a security guard in her building. It happens to be the same complex where Dev lived.'

'And she knew Dev well, I gather?'

'Yes, ma'am. They were in a relationship.'

She shook her head. 'That man was incorrigible.'

A question came to Kabir's mind, something he had wondered about even earlier, but he refrained from asking it. Instead, he said carefully, 'We had initially suspected that she could be behind the murder of Dev Malik but not any more.'

'What do you mean?'

'Well, we now have strong reason to believe that Neena Razdan had hired the boy Irfan to kill her husband and not Dev Malik.'

'I don't understand, Kabir.' The commissioner frowned. 'Explain.'

Kabir took a deep breath and narrated the sequence of events, from his first meeting with Neena to the scene at her apartment after Irfan's death and then her interrogation at the Crime Branch headquarters.

The commissioner interrupted. 'Why wasn't this woman investigated earlier?'

'Honestly, she seemed a little unstable to me. But I didn't think she was capable of cold, calculated murder.' Kabir sighed. 'As it turns out, I was quite wrong, ma'am.'

'Go on.'

'We questioned her husband this morning, just before I came here. It turns out that not only was their marriage on the rocks, but Neena had even threatened a few times to kill him.'

'Why didn't he report it to the police?'

'He said that he didn't think she would actually do anything. However, on one occasion, he accidentally discovered on their home computer's search history that Neena had been googling for "poisons that can't be detected" and "how to kill someone when they're sleeping".'

The commissioner gave a wry smile. 'She wouldn't be the first woman to have murderous thoughts about her husband, I can tell you that.'

Kabir continued, 'In fact, Irfan had accosted him early one morning when he was out for a walk. Given all that happened later, the husband feels that it could have been an attempt on his life, but luckily for him, something scared the boy off at the last minute.'

'That's all very circumstantial, Kabir.'

'Yes, ma'am, you're right. So we decided to interrogate Neena Razdan again, this time about her husband.' Kabir paused. 'She just confessed to everything.'

'And you believe her?'

'I do because she had two strong motives to kill him. She's his only next of kin and stood to get a lot of money and their apartment if he died. That's apart from the fact that she caught him having an affair with a colleague.'

The commissioner rolled her eyes. 'A couple made for each other. Anyway, what exactly happened?'

'Neena Razdan had figured out that Irfan was a fellow with few morals and a penchant for violence. She paid him to bump off her husband, making it look like a mugging gone wrong. We don't know exactly why Irfan didn't go through with the hit, but he still wanted his money and tried to blackmail Neena to get it.'

'So that's why she decided to kill him instead.'

Kabir nodded. 'Yes, ma'am. Though I don't think it was premeditated. Irfan came up to Neena's apartment that evening and threatened her, which is when all this happened.'

'So you're back to square one, Kabir.' The commissioner leaned back in her chair. 'What about the original suspect, Dev's girlfriend?'

'Sharon Sequeira. We…'

Just then, his phone rang. It was SI Patil. Kabir knew that it had to be urgent, otherwise Patil wouldn't have interrupted his meeting with the commissioner.

After a brief conversation, Kabir looked up and said, 'We… we've finally located Sharon Sequeira, ma'am.'

29

Sharon Sequeira lay on the white hospital bed, strapped onto a ventilator with tubes in her nose and mouth. Though she was in a state of deep unconsciousness, the blue monitor screen showed that her vitals were steady.

Her hair was cropped short, almost into a buzz cut. A bandage, stained red and yellow, covered her forehead. Her face was gaunt, almost emaciated, and there were dark circles under her eyes. The blue sheet covering her body below the neck concealed the serious injuries she had suffered in the accident.

There were four broken ribs, thankfully none of which had punctured a lung. The impact on the steering wheel had caused major abdominal trauma and heavy bleeding. One shoulder was badly dislocated. It was clear that Sharon hadn't been wearing a seat belt when the collision happened.

A trauma surgeon was brought in from one of the large multispeciality hospitals in Navi Mumbai, for the patient wasn't in any state to be moved. He operated on her for over six hours and repaired as best as he could the damage inside her body cavity, but the brain injuries were another matter.

The front part of Sharon's skull was fractured at the point where it had struck the windscreen. There were multiple contusions and severe haemorrhaging inside. Some of the blood had been taken out through a hole drilled near the top of her head, but beyond that, the doctors couldn't do anything but wait.

Mrs Sequeira stood next to her daughter's bed, tears streaming down her face. 'My poor... baby. How could this... have happened?'

When she got the call about Sharon having been located, her initial euphoria had given way to despair after she learnt that her daughter was in a critical condition and barely alive. She tried calling Rhea Menon several times, but there was no response. In fact, Rhea had been incommunicado for a few days, which was very unusual for her.

There was no one else to accompany her. So Mrs Sequeira hailed a taxi and gave the driver the address of the hospital in Panvel. The drive took an agonising couple of hours, during which she prayed continuously with a rosary in her hand. When she finally reached, Sharon had just been wheeled out of the operation theatre after the marathon surgery.

'I'm really sorry,' said the surgeon, who was still in his scrubs. 'Things don't look good for her, unfortunately.'

'Will she... live, doctor?'

'Well, she's been in a bad car accident. Her injuries are extensive.' A nurse handed him some papers on a clipboard. He glanced at them with an expert eye and scribbled something. 'Her body will heal with time, but I'm very worried about the intracranial trauma. It's a miracle that she survived in the first place.'

'Can I... at least... speak to her?'

He shook his head. 'The patient is in a deep coma, I'm afraid. It's impossible to predict what will happen next. She could recover in a few weeks or never wake up at all.'

'What are... her chances?'

'I can't really say. Medical science hasn't yet understood the workings of the human brain fully. But there's no doubt that her condition is very fragile.'

Mrs Sequeira grasped his hand tightly with both of hers and sobbed, 'Please... save my girl, doctor. I... beg you.'

The surgeon patted her on the shoulder and smiled ruefully. 'We'll try, ma'am. Let's hope for the best.'

He gently led Mrs Sequeira out of the ICU, where a number of policemen were waiting.

SI Patil stepped up and said softly, 'I know this is a very difficult time, Mrs Sequeira, but we really need to talk.'

Back at the Crime Branch headquarters, there was plenty of activity. After receiving the call from SI Patil, Kabir rushed from the commissioner's office and directed various lines of enquiry in the wake of finally locating Sharon Sequeira. Just as the realisation dawned that Neena Razdan was a dead end, at least in the Dev Malik murder, the investigation had sprung back to life.

Kabir knew that he had to make the most of this lucky break. The probe had veered in different directions, but the discovery of Sharon alive, suddenly made her the prime suspect once again. Not only was it established that she had been at Dev's apartment that night, but it was now clear that she had a strong motive as well. All that remained was to build a watertight case against her.

A forensics mobile unit was dispatched to the accident spot in Khandala to check if any evidence had been missed. The sub-inspector who had first surveyed the scene and identified the injured woman was summoned. This time, he brimmed with energy and self-importance, knowing that he had played a role in potentially solving a high-profile crime from the metropolis.

Too much time had passed, however, and the only remaining testament to the accident was the jamun tree into which the car had crashed. The sturdy trunk had withstood the collision, though a big wedge had come off and the bark was badly lacerated. There were scrapes of white paint and some pieces of glass still lying around. Leaves and clumps of fruit had fallen to the ground from the impact.

The team fanned out through the trees in a large radius, looking for anything that might be linked to the accident, but they drew a blank. Since all the tyre tracks had virtually disappeared, they had to depend on the sub-inspector's report from his initial visit, which he happily described again, embellishing his detection skills considerably in the narration. However, he forgot to mention his observation about the surprisingly limited damage to the car, considering the high-speed collision with the tree.

The truck driver who had brought Sharon to the police outpost was still in detention and despite multiple rounds of questioning, steadfastly maintained that he hadn't taken any of the woman's belongings. The bus driver who had discovered the accident was nowhere to be found. The police only wanted to get a first-hand account from him and he wasn't a suspect, but knowing the ways of law enforcement in the country, he had decided to disappear for a while.

A couple of constables were at the nearby toll plaza, reviewing the CCTV footage. The white car had passed through just after one o'clock the previous night. It was evident that the driver was the only occupant of the vehicle. Her head was covered with a peaked cap and her face wasn't clearly visible, but her scar could be seen even in the grainy video. It could be none other than Sharon Sequeira, they figured.

On a hunch, one of the constables decided to check the footage from the other side of the highway. It bore fruit, for the vehicle had indeed driven through from the opposite direction just over three hours earlier. There was another toll booth some distance away, but she hadn't gone through it, which meant that she would have turned off somewhere.

It became clear that Sharon Sequeira had driven to some specific destination in the vicinity and was returning from there when the accident happened. The area had a couple of villages, some resorts and several vacation homes; and it was decided that the local thana would send their men around to make enquiries. The car was a standard-issue rental and quite nondescript, but maybe someone might remember seeing the tall woman with curly hair.

Meanwhile in Mumbai, a Crime Branch team was at the car agency office. Sharon Sequeira had hired the self-drive vehicle with a cash deposit the day after Dev's murder. There was no doubt it was her, for she had submitted a copy of her driving licence. No CCTV footage was available, though the man who had taken the booking testified that he had confirmed the woman's face with the photo on the licence.

The vehicle wasn't fitted with a GPS system so there was no way to track where it had been driven. However, its odometer would show that it had clocked over five hundred kilometres after being rented by Sharon Sequeira. A bulletin was sent out with the description and registration number to check if the car might have passed through any other toll point, or been spotted at a gas station, or served a challan for a traffic violation, but it was a long shot.

The agency proprietor swore that the car had been in great condition. Not only had it been serviced recently, but the brakes and tyres had both been replaced. So there was no question of any mechanical fault having caused the accident. It had to be a driver's error. 'Was she drunk?' he asked. The police didn't bother telling him that there had been no trace of alcohol in Sharon Sequeira's blood.

The wrecked car was towed all the way to the Worli thana, where Nusrat was waiting with a forensics team. Despite what the rental agency claimed, it would have to be sent later to the police workshop for a full mechanical check-up, but the first priority was to make sure that no evidence was lost.

There was plenty of dried blood on the driver's seat and dashboard, which they sampled for DNA analysis, though it would have almost certainly come from Sharon Sequeira. At the spot where her head had hit the windscreen, the laminated glass had a spider web-like crack but no blood. *That woman must have a really hard skull*, Nusrat thought.

The interior of the car was absolutely devoid of any of her belongings or even the usual items like receipts, food wrappers, water bottles and so on. Nusrat was puzzled. It was very strange for anyone to have been moving around without a phone or money or ID, even a killer on the run. The only explanation was that someone had cleaned out the vehicle after the accident.

There were traces of blood and hair at the back as well, which were meticulously photographed and collected. It was true that an unconscious Sharon had been pulled out through the rear door, but the pattern couldn't be explained just by that. It seemed like she had been lying down in the space between the front and rear seats at some point and bled through minor cuts. The DNA analysis would reveal in due course whether that had been a different person entirely.

There were a number of fingerprints inside and outside the vehicle, which the team carefully lifted and bagged as part of the procedure. Nusrat knew it wouldn't help them much, for most of the prints were likely to be Sharon's and the others could belong to practically anybody, making identification almost impossible. *Still, if there are any twists later, this evidence will come in handy.*

The mechanism to open the trunk had somehow jammed during the collision, so a metal-cutter was used to open it. At first glance, there was nothing out of the ordinary inside, just a spare tyre, a toolkit and an old plastic bottle. It was only when the matting was peeled back that they finally got lucky. Hidden beneath it was a kitchen knife with deep brown streaks. Nusrat knew instinctively that she was staring at the weapon which had been used to kill Dev Malik.

She immediately called Kabir and said excitedly, 'Sir, I think we've hit the jackpot!'

'That's great, Nusrat. What have you found?'

'We'll have to wait for the DNA results and fingerprint analysis, but it's the murder weapon. I'm quite certain.'

She described her examination of the car, and finding the knife in the trunk.

'You must be right, Nusrat. It would be too much of a coincidence otherwise.'

'Yes, sir. It looks like we were always on the right track with Sharon Sequeira as our original suspect. If only we had managed to find her earlier...'

'Police work needs some luck, Nusrat. We just got our share of it late in the investigation.'

'So what? You managed to solve another crime in the process, sir.' There was admiration in Nusrat's voice.

'Neena Razdan, you mean?'

'Yes, sir. If she wasn't interrogated as a suspect in the Dev Malik murder, then it's quite likely that she might have gotten away with her version of having killed the security guard in self-defence.'

'I don't know, Nusrat. The law would have eventually caught up with her.'

'Anyway, we're finally going to crack this case now!'

'Yes, I think we will.' Kabir paused. 'And there's one more thing.'

'What's that, sir?'

'You remember I had asked you to get the hair we found on Harry Shah's body analysed for the DNA of Sharon Sequeira?'

'Don't tell me…'

'Yes, Nusrat. I just got a call from the FSL. It's a match. So we now have Sharon as the likely killer of Harry Shah as well.'

30

POLICE SOLVE WORLI MURDERS

Mumbai: The sensational murders of socialite Dev Malik and businessman Harry Shah have been solved by the Mumbai Police. Both lived in Ocean West, a luxury residential complex in Worli which is home to several prominent citizens. While Dev was stabbed to death in his own apartment, Harry was found in Aarey Colony with his head bludgeoned.

Sharon Sequeira, a dentist by profession and Dev's girlfriend, has been named as the prime accused in both cases. Police claim that she killed Dev in a fit of jealousy after learning that he was cheating on her. Harry, Dev's neighbour, was a witness to the crime and tried to blackmail her, whereupon she lured him to Aarey and killed him as well.

After Dev's murder, Ms Sequeira went absconding for several days. It has now come to light that she had gone into hiding in Khandala and is in police custody after her car met with an accident on the Mumbai–Pune Highway. She suffered serious injuries in the collision and remains in critical condition.

DCP Kabir Khan of the Crime Branch said, 'We are pleased to have concluded this important investigation. Sharon Sequeira was our primary suspect from the beginning and we have enough evidence against her, including CCTV footage and the knife used to stab Dev Malik. DNA evidence places her conclusively at both murder scenes and there is no further doubt that she is the killer.'

Friends and family of Ms Sequeira are in a state of shock. According to a neighbour who doesn't wish to be named, 'I can't believe Sharon did this. She's such a nice and straightforward girl. It's impossible to imagine that she can take a human life, let alone two. The police have found a convenient scapegoat to close the case without bothering to get to the bottom of it.'

Dev Malik's estranged wife, well-known actress and television personality Tanya B, refused to comment on the developments.

The editor of the city's premier news daily found the article draft too dry but approved it anyway. He had decided to put it on the front page but still needed a photo of Sharon Sequeira. After all, a story on what could be the crime of the decade was incomplete without his readers being able to visualise the killer, especially when it happened to be a beautiful woman.

Dev Malik's death had certainly made news, but when the circumstances of his murder and its aftermath were revealed, the media went into a frenzy. While Dev's life was largely in the public domain, little was known about Sharon and Harry. Neither had any presence on social platforms, and every agency scrambled to find out more about them the old-fashioned way.

Parallels were drawn to the 1959 case of Commander Nanavati, the naval officer who had shot dead his wife's lover after discovering her infidelity but was eventually pardoned by the state governor Vijayalakshmi Pandit, sister of Jawaharlal Nehru. The incident received unprecedented press coverage at the time and continues to inspire books and films even sixty years later.

Mrs Sequeira managed to get out with her grandson and move into an apartment in Vashi owned by her brother, the dentist from Pune who had inspired Sharon to take up the same profession. Not only did she escape the news crews who camped outside their Khar building, but it put her much closer to the hospital where Sharon was admitted, albeit with very little hope of survival.

Not surprisingly, there was plenty of support and sympathy for Sharon. Many women perceived her as the victim and applauded her courage. The fact that she was in a coma and fighting for her life made it difficult for her to be portrayed as a ruthless killer. A dais set up in front of the hospital by an NGO was soon full of candles, flowers and cards wishing Sharon a speedy recovery.

Intense debates raged on social media, arguing the morality versus the legality of the case. Sharon had certainly broken the law by taking two human lives but was the provocation justified? Most media houses were on her side, sensing public sentiment, and widely featured Sharon's acquaintances as well as independent commentators speaking out in her favour. Besides, they gleefully laid bare not only Dev's sexual shenanigans but also Harry Shah's shady past.

The Mumbai Police, however, took a dim view of all the media chatter and were determined to bring Sharon Sequeira to justice.

'Nice to see you enjoying your lunch, for a change.' Kabir had a grin on his face.

His mouth stuffed with hakka noodles and chilli chicken, Patil could only nod vigorously in agreement. They were at the Worli thana, where he had ordered in simple but delicious Chinese fare for everyone in the station to celebrate the solving of the Ocean West murders.

'Don't I deserve it, sir!'

'Yes, certainly. I'm glad we wrapped things up quickly.'

Nearly seventy-two hours had gone by since the identification of Sharon Sequeira as the woman from the accident. Further review of CCTV footage from the toll plaza revealed that she had driven through it a number of times over the past few days. The Khandala Police hadn't yet figured out where she had been holed up, but it didn't matter.

DNA analysis of the knife found in the car had come back in record time, confirming Sharon's fingerprints and Dev's blood on it. That, combined with the presence of her hair on Harry Shah's corpse, was enough for an indictment. A round-the-clock police picket was posted outside the hospital, but Sharon wasn't going anywhere.

'We won't get to arrest Ms Sequeira, sir.' Patil covered his mouth and belched audibly. 'Her condition has deteriorated further. The doctors don't think she'll live out the week.'

Kabir pointed upwards. 'Looks like the Almighty has meted out punishment already.'

'It would have been nice to have interrogated her and got a confession.'

'I don't know about that, Harish. With so much press attention, it could have become tricky for us.'

'Maybe you're right. Some greedy lawyer would have convinced her to maintain her innocence and let the trial play out in the media.' He immediately looked contrite. 'Sorry, no offence meant, sir.'

'None taken.' Kabir smiled. 'My parents are practically retired anyway.'

After a pause, Patil said, 'I would still like to know what exactly happened at Dev Malik's apartment that evening, sir. Was Ms Sequeira jealous and angry enough to have gone there with an intent to kill or did it occur in the heat of the moment?'

'I would have said it's the latter but for what happened with Harry Shah later. That was cold-blooded murder.'

'It surprises me how Ms Sequeira managed to evade us for so long, sir. Switching off her phone, renting a car with cash, finding a hideout outside the city... She acted like a seasoned felon.'

'She didn't call any of her close relatives and friends either, right?'

'No, sir. We were tracking that. First-time criminals usually panic and try to seek help or refuge from known people. And yet, Ms Sequeira was calm enough not to do that.'

'She's a smart and intelligent woman. Her survival instincts must have kicked in quickly.'

'She did make one mistake, sir. Her credit card was used at a supermarket in Navi Mumbai some days back. Even though we had hotlisted it, the bank never informed us due to some glitch in their back end.'

'The car accident was her second mistake, Harish. Without that, we may not have caught up with her.'

Patil rolled his eyes. 'She couldn't have remained in hiding forever.'

Kabir looked thoughtful. 'I wonder if she had an accomplice. Maybe the mystery woman who had sent her the photos? We still don't know who that was.'

'I guess we'll never find out, sir.'

'The one thing that confounds me is why Sharon decided to murder Harry Shah. She hadn't made any secret of visiting Dev's apartment that evening. The security guards had seen her, and there was CCTV footage too. What else did Harry know that led to his death?'

'Maybe he had seen her in the act of stabbing Dev?'

'I suppose that's possible. But I think it was something else, Harish. She must have known that she would be the prime suspect in Dev's murder. Why take the risk of contacting Harry several times and then killing him in a public place?'

'Only Ms Sequeira can tell us, sir.'

'Anyway, we have a strong motive, compelling DNA evidence, and her presence confirmed at both crime scenes.'

Kabir shrugged. 'That's what the court needs, even if we never come to know all the facts of the case.'

Patil smiled. 'As they say, all's well that ends well.'

'My daughter is completely innocent, and nothing the police say can change that.' Mrs Sequeira's face was haggard, but her voice was firm. 'The person who actually committed these murders has framed Sharon and even tried to kill her. It's only by the grace of our Lord that she's still alive.'

'Why did she go into hiding then, ma'am?'

'Who says she went into hiding?' Mrs Sequeira took a sip of water and continued, 'She was abducted, that's what happened! If only the police could stop making her the scapegoat and start investigating properly, then…'

Minnie got up and switched off the television.

She had always wondered how Harry figured out that it was her and not Sharon at Dev's apartment that night, and he never let on either. It was actually the distinctive tattoo she had on her neck. A stylised version of the Scorpio symbol that looked like an M, denoting her name as well. M for Minnie.

She made herself a gin and tonic. She didn't drink alcohol that often any more but suddenly felt like celebrating. After all, it had been a tumultuous few days, and everything finally fell into place. Her last worry was gone. Well, almost. There was one loose end still remaining.

Minnie raised an imaginary toast and began laughing hysterically.

31

Tanya was sick and tired of all the press attention the case was getting.

Every newspaper, channel and website had reached out to her for a sound byte or an interview, but she had steadfastly refused, knowing that the questions would invariably centre on her relationship with Dev and the significant others in their respective lives. It hadn't stopped them from writing about her anyway, twisting the facts salaciously for a city fed on Bollywood masala.

A horde of reporters and camera-persons waited outside the gate of her apartment complex, ready to ambush her. *This has become a circus,* she thought angrily. She knew the media would eventually move on to something else, but there was no doubt that the murders, and more so the murderess, had the entire nation gripped in morbid fascination.

SI Patil had come by personally to apprise her of the dramatic developments. His opening words were,

'We've found her, ma'am... Ms Sharon Sequeira. Your husband's killer.'

Tanya's face was impassive, betraying no emotion. She had already heard the news, of course.

Beaming, Patil continued, 'There's enough evidence to prove beyond doubt that she's the culprit.'

'I heard there was a second murder as well?'

'Yes, Harry Shah. Dev's neighbour. I believe you would have known him, ma'am?'

Tanya shook her head. 'I don't think so.'

'I see.' Patil frowned. As far as he knew, Harry Shah had been residing in Ocean West for over a year. 'Anyway, it looks like he was blackmailing Ms Sequeira.'

'What about?'

'We don't know that yet, ma'am. But it's definitely connected to Dev somehow.'

'You do have proof that she killed him as well?'

'That's correct.'

There was silence for a few moments. Then Patil got up reluctantly and said, 'I need to go now, ma'am. Don't hesitate to call me if you need anything.'

'Thank you, inspector.' Tanya touched his arm. 'This won't bring Dev back, but it definitely gives me some closure.'

Patil nodded. Just as he turned around to leave, she asked, 'One last thing. Is that woman going to live?'

'I'm afraid not, ma'am.' He sighed. 'It looks like justice has been served anyway.'

Kabir sat at his desk, a thoughtful expression on his face. It was almost lunchtime, but strangely, he didn't feel hungry.

One fact continued to bother him about the Dev Malik case. *Why had Sharon Sequeira kept the knife in the car?* She had been smart enough to escape detection from the entire police force of the state for so many days, yet she had made such an obvious and grave mistake. It would have been so easy to dispose of it anywhere in the jungles along the highway, and no one would have ever known.

It was common knowledge that the murder weapon was the most incriminating piece of evidence for nailing a killer. Yet, Sharon had chosen to keep the knife in her car, where it was certain to be found. It was possible that she had meant to get rid of it later but had forgotten. However, everything else had been carefully cleared out from the car, leaving no trace behind.

Kabir picked up his phone and dialled SI Patil.

'Good afternoon, sir.'

'Harish, did the Khandala Police find out where Sharon Sequeira was coming from when the accident happened?'

Patil was taken aback. 'You still have something in your mind, sir?'

'Just tying up a loose end.'

'Let me check.'

He called back in half an hour. 'Looks like we have something, sir.'

'Go on.'

'Not too far from the toll booth, there's a diversion from the highway. It joins up a narrow road going up the hillside. A man who owns a small tea shop at that corner saw a white car go by sometime after midnight. Though he doesn't remember the make of the car, it slowed down while passing, as there's a speed breaker at the spot, and he noticed that the driver was a woman wearing a cap.'

'Sharon Sequeira.'

'Yes, sir. It must have been her. The place and time are a match too.'

'But Harish, how does this help determine where she was coming from?'

'I was getting to that. The man told us that the road goes on for five kilometres and ends up at Mount Serenity, a luxury villa property. There's pretty much nothing else there, not even a village. Just dense forest.'

'Did the team visit the place?'

'Actually no, sir. The case is already solved, right?'

Kabir hung up without saying another word. He walked out and fired up his Bullet, setting course for Khandala.

Ninety minutes later, Kabir stopped in front of the large signboard of Mount Serenity. He knew the builder well, for they were an important client of his parents and had even offered him a prime land parcel there at a throwaway price. It was tempting, but Kabir knew that he was too much of a city boy to really make use of such a getaway.

The arched gates were open, and Kabir drove on to the makeshift guard house inside. Seeing him, a dark man in a khaki shirt and dirty trousers stumbled out. Staring at Kabir with bloodshot eyes, he asked, 'Whom do you want?'

Kabir replied with a cold glare, 'I'm from the Crime Branch, Mumbai Police.'

The man straightened and saluted clumsily. He was clearly inebriated.

Kabir asked disbelievingly, 'You're in charge of security?'

'Yes, sir. I mean… No, I do odd jobs at the site, sir. The guards haven't come today, the lazy wretches, so… The supervisor asked me to sit here, sir.'

'Where is your supervisor?'

'He's gone to the city today, sir. I… don't know when he will return.'

'Doesn't anyone live here now?'

'All construction has stopped for many months, sir. There's some… problem with building permissions. Only a few houses are ready but… no one comes.'

'Are you sure?'

The man hesitated for a couple of moments, then said, 'Actually, there is someone… who comes and stays here sometimes. He has some type of outhouse on one of the plots.'

Kabir said impatiently, 'Show me.'

Somehow, the old man wasn't surprised to see a police officer show up at the doorstep of his little gazebo. He looked around dramatically, as if to check if anyone was watching, before ushering Kabir inside.

'I'm so glad you're here,' he began excitedly.

'Why?'

'I think... no, I'm sure... There's something illegal going on here.' He pointed outside vaguely.

Kabir showed him a photo of Sharon Sequeira on his phone. 'Have you seen this woman?'

The old man got up and picked up a pair of reading glasses from the small writing table. 'Hmm... No, I don't think so.'

'All right then. Tell me what's bothering you.'

Kabir listened carefully as the man narrated the sequence of events, starting with the strange midnight arrival of his neighbour several days ago. The night of Dev Malik's murder. He took out his notebook and jotted down the times and dates of her visits, which the man remembered in great detail. Age certainly hadn't dimmed his mind.

'What was the colour of her car?' Kabir asked finally.

'She used to have a bigger, dark-coloured vehicle earlier, but this one was white.'

The man couldn't tell him the licence plate number, since she would always come in after dark, but there was no doubt in Kabir's mind that it was the rental car Sharon had been found in. He got up and walked to the windows.

'It's the yellow villa opposite, right?'

'Yes, sir.'

'Does any caretaker live there?'

'I've never seen anyone except her.'

'Given your testimony, we'll need to search the house.' Kabir looked thoughtful. 'I forgot to ask. What's her name? Do you know?'

The man brightened. 'Yes, of course. Didn't I mention it before? It's Tanya B, the actress.'

Suddenly the room seemed to spin. 'Tanya?' Kabir's voice was incredulous.

'Yes, sir. it's her place. She's even smiled at me a few times.' He looked sheepish. 'I mean, not recently. Much earlier.'

'And it was Tanya who was coming here in the white car?'

'That's the thing, sir. I didn't see her clearly so I can't be absolutely sure.' The man looked serious suddenly. 'Do you think it's someone else, and something's happened to Tanya?'

Kabir shook his head. 'No, I know for a fact that she's fine.'

Suddenly, things began to fall into place. *We've been getting this wrong all along.* It was no coincidence that Tanya's name had come up in this manner. She had to be the woman the old man had seen. There was no way Sharon Sequeira would have driven up to Tanya's hill home after murdering Dev Malik unless the two had conspired together to kill him. *That was out of the question,* Kabir thought. *Everything was fine between Dev and Sharon until a few hours before his death.*

It was far more likely that Tanya had somehow set up Sharon. Maybe she was the woman who had called her at the clinic that fateful day and sent the photographs as well. *Was it plain jealousy?* Kabir wondered. *Hell hath no fury like a woman scorned.* Kabir remembered Nusrat's suspicions about Tanya, and her theory that she had bumped off one of her past boyfriends.

And yet, all the evidence was stacked against Sharon, in both the murders of Dev and Harry. From her presence at both crime scenes to the discovery of the murder weapons, it was like a textbook indictment. *And that's always been the problem with this case.* Everything was too obvious, pointing too clearly to one person, who was as unlikely a killer as they come.

Kabir closed his eyes. He remembered his first meeting with Tanya at Dev's apartment. Something had bothered him about the conversation, but he hadn't been able to put his finger to it. With the increasing likelihood that Sharon Sequeira was guilty and the subsequent events with Harry Shah and Neena Razdan, he hadn't followed up on his instincts. *A big mistake.*

In fact, Kabir had subconsciously registered the hard edge in Tanya's personality. It was like a coldness towards death, something he had seen in people who could kill without remorse. Not that it necessarily made her a murderer or was any kind of evidence, but he realised that he shouldn't have dropped her as a suspect so early in the investigation.

At that moment, Kabir knew without a doubt that Dev's killer was none other than Tanya. Every cell in him screamed that it had to be her. He couldn't fathom exactly how or why she had done it, and maybe he never would. She was obviously a very smart woman and had hatched an elaborate plan to frame Sharon. It all seemed to have gone perfectly. With Harry dead and Sharon out of the way, there was no one to testify against Tanya.

He sighed and got up. 'Thank you for your help. We'll look into this further.'

The old man smiled briefly and said, 'There's one more thing. The house is registered in Tanya's real name, *Minnie Bose.*

32

It was only by chance that Tanya found out about Dev's infidelity.

She knew of his past of course, though he never told her the actual number of women he had slept with in his entire life. It would have shocked her. Tanya naively assumed that Dev had already sown his wild oats, and settled down with her. There was certainly a lot of passion and romance in their marriage.

It happened as it so often does. Tanya was up late one night, sitting in the drawing room and rehearsing her lines for an important shoot the next day. Dev was fast asleep inside. There was a beep, and she saw that he had left his mobile phone charging on the bar cabinet. On an impulse, she picked it up.

The message preview was brief, and Tanya's face blanched as she read it. It was a question really, asking Dev when his wife was going to next leave town. The phone was locked so she couldn't open the app and see the entire conversation, but the series of heart emojis left no doubt as to what the sender meant.

The rage would come later when she would investigate further and discover the sheer scale of his philandering. It would appear that marriage hadn't made any difference to him at all. But at that moment, she felt strangely calm.

There was only one thought in her mind. *Not again.*

As a child, Minnie used to have sudden bouts of explosive anger which made her scream shrilly, break objects, or hit whoever was nearby. Her parents dismissed them as growing-up tantrums and later, hormonal changes. A doctor friend told them that this was not uncommon in exceptionally intelligent children like Minnie, whose fast-developing minds often experienced high levels of anxiety.

The episodes didn't stop even when she entered her teens, but Minnie managed to prevent their manifestations by locking herself in a room or running out of the house whenever it happened. Gradually, she learnt to control the anger itself and direct the energy back at its root cause, often violently. A cold, hard spot emerged inside Minnie's psyche; and she felt no remorse in getting back at anyone who she felt had wronged her. *I'm a true, vengeful Scorpio,* she would keep telling herself.

Minnie faced the first major consequence of her actions when she lost her job after breaking the nose of the executive who had made a pass at her. She felt no guilt or regret, for the man had it coming, but it taught her that she needed to be more careful. She later managed to stay clear of Sunny Gupta's death with a lot of manipulation and some luck but knew that battles would have to be picked in future.

Especially after she joined the entertainment industry, full of lechers and charlatans, Minnie realised that it would be impossible to survive unless she developed a thick skin. The first thing she did was change her name. Minnie sounded like the girl next door and wasn't suitable for her public persona. It was her producer who suggested Tanya, which was both sexy and mysterious.

Khuki's death had a profound impact on Tanya. Losing her beloved, baby sister in such a manner was a terrible shock in itself, but the fact that her killer was never caught was something Tanya found very difficult to accept. In her mind, she had failed Khuki miserably, first in protecting her and then in avenging her.

When Tanya discovered that Dev was not only cheating on her but had been doing so for a while and with multiple women, something snapped inside her. Her love for him made way for a deep, burning hatred. To her, Dev suddenly became the embodiment of every man who had ever wronged a woman, including the stranger who was responsible for Khuki's death. *Not to mention her own father.*

She decided that Dev had lost the right to live.

Tanya forced herself to remain calm when she confronted Dev about his affairs. She couldn't let him get any inkling of what was raging through her mind. He didn't deny the accusations but begged her to give him a second chance. In the end, she pretended to consider but insisted that they needed a period of separation to think things through. However, there was one thing she needed to do before leaving the apartment.

Tanya had first heard of mobile spying software from a friend who had installed it on her teenage daughter's phone to keep tabs on her. With such an app, one could read messages, monitor GPS locations, log call details and websites visited, and view photos, emails and contacts—all without the knowledge of the mobile user. It took Tanya just a day to figure out the screen unlock password on Dev's iPhone and install the software. The next morning, she left.

By then, Dev had already started going out with Sharon, and Tanya was aware of the fact. In a stark departure from his usual flings, he was apparently quite serious about her, but Tanya needed to see that for herself. One evening, she followed Dev as he drove to Sharon's clinic, picked her up and went to a lounge bar in Parel. The place was dimly lit and had two levels so Tanya was able to get a table for herself and observe them without being spotted. The intimacy between the two was obvious. But even as her blazing eyes checked out every detail about Sharon, an idea began forming in Tanya's mind.

First, she needed to find out more about the woman, which she did simply by snooping on Dev's phone chats with her. The resentment Tanya felt at reading the passionate exchanges only served to strengthen her resolve. For the initial part of her plan, she knew that she had to be patient and wait for Dev to provide an opportunity, which she was certain he would do sooner or later. The fact that it turned out to be with Rhea Menon, Sharon's best friend, was an incredible bonus, but somehow, Tanya wasn't surprised.

After that, Tanya prepared meticulously for the second and final acts. She got in touch with a 'fixer' close to one of her producers, a useful if unsavoury contact, and obtained a handgun, an untraceable mobile phone, handcuffs and leg irons, some chloroform and an injectable knockout drug, among other items. The knife she procured on her own, along with a set of wine glasses. She then went to her trusted make-up artist, showed him a photo and gave him detailed instructions. Shortlisting of the car rental agency, a visit to Khandala to keep things ready there, and the stage was set.

When Tanya saw the message from Dev inviting Sharon for dinner at the apartment, she knew it was time. Putting the pill into Jeet's bottle of whisky would ensure her alibi for later, for he would be too disoriented to remember that she was out all evening.

Reeling in Sharon was easy, from sending the photos to make her jealous to luring her to the rendezvous in Bandra. After getting into her car, Tanya quickly brandished the gun and as Sharon froze, she thrust the wad of chloroform in her face. There was a brief but violent struggle, for both women were strong; however, as the chloroform took over, Sharon soon passed out.

Tanya quickly attached dark blinds on the car windows and went to work. She took off Sharon's dress and put it on; as expected, it was a perfect fit. The curly wig and a fake scar, to impersonate Sharon's most distinctive features, completed the look. Tanya knew the resemblance was strong enough to deceive most people and certainly CCTV cameras. She started the car and drove towards Ocean West. Sharon lay unconscious on the back seat, covered with a shapeless black canvas sheet.

As soon as she entered the apartment, Tanya took off her wig and smiled at Dev. He stared at her, dumbfounded. Without saying a word, she walked past him and sat on a sofa in the drawing room, putting her large handbag on the centre table. Dev followed her, finally finding his voice. 'You? Where's... Sharon?'

In reply, she pulled him towards her and kissed him on the mouth. Dev reflexively kissed her back, then pushed her away and said, 'Wait! What are you doing here?'

'I... just wanted us to make love one last time, Dev.'

'No... I...'

She kissed him again and pushed him firmly down on the carpet. Pinning him with her knees, Tanya took off her dress in a smooth motion. She was naked underneath, and Dev couldn't help feeling a stirring in his loins. Sex with Tanya had always been terrific. She put a finger on his lips and held up a black silk scarf in her other hand. He didn't resist, for it was one of his favourite kinks.

When Tanya carefully drove the knife between two ribs into his lung, a blindfolded Dev was too shocked to react for a moment. He opened his mouth to scream, but she immediately covered his face with a cushion and stabbed him two more times in quick succession. He shuddered once and then lay still, even as a pool of crimson widened around his lifeless body.

Tanya closed her eyes and took a deep breath, willing her heart to stop pounding. Then she got up and went to the kitchen for the first in a sequence of actions she had prepared meticulously and rehearsed in her mind several times. The knife she used to kill Dev was part of a set identical to the one she had bought for their household a few months earlier. Putting on a pair of gloves, Tanya removed it from the rack on the kitchen top and put it in her bag.

Next, she took a tumbler from the cabinet and placed Dev's inert hand around it, before pouring in a peg of whisky. She opened the bottle of Riesling that was chilling in the fridge and poured some into the wine glass already smudged with Sharon's fingerprints, that she had brought along with her. The glass was the same make as a set Dev kept in his bar.

She removed Dev's blindfold and stared at his handsome face, now pale and contorted in death. She felt no remorse or sadness. *He deserved this.* Tanya didn't bother wiping her own fingerprints, for she had made sure to visit the apartment only a few days earlier. Donning her wig again, she took a final look around and left.

At that time of night, it took her just over two hours to reach the villa in Khandala. As they entered, Sharon suddenly came to and groaned faintly. Tanya hit her hard on the head and dragged her to the guest room, where she secured her to the foot of the heavy four-poster bed with the steel restraints she had brought along. The windows anyway had blackout curtains for extra privacy.

The plan was to keep Sharon alive for a couple of days to make it appear that she had gone into hiding after murdering Dev. Tanya was aware that it increased the risk for her, but she was counting on the fact it would establish

Sharon's guilt beyond any shade of doubt. Until that point, everything had gone without a hitch.

The next morning, Tanya received a call from an unknown number. The caller was Harry Shah and Tanya's face fell when she heard what he had to say.

Despite what she told SI Patil later, Tanya had met Harry a couple of times. She didn't know him too well but had heard he was a dubious character. There was also a rumour going around that he was deep in debt, and desperately needed money; which explained why he didn't go to the police and decided to blackmail her instead.

When the initial panic subsided, Tanya began to think clearly. She figured that with some planning and a little bit of luck, she could even turn the situation to her advantage. However, it meant that Sharon would have to be kept alive longer. *No matter, it's a small price to pay for the joy of pinning two murders on that bitch.*

After pretending to be outraged at his accusation, she asked Harry to prove what he was saying, but he insisted that he couldn't do that over the phone. Tanya knew a meeting would be risky so she strung him along for a few days and then called him to the early morning tryst at Aarey, where she killed him. Trusting the forensic skills of the police, she placed Sharon's hair on Harry's corpse to implicate her.

Tanya's only fear was that he might have told someone else or that the police had found out somehow. When

Nusrat came to her sets to enquire about Sunny Gupta, her heart had missed a beat. She wasn't worried about that old incident for there was absolutely nothing to link her to it. But for a few moments, Tanya wondered if it was leading up to connecting her to Dev's murder as well. However, it soon became clear that wasn't the case.

After disposing of Harry, she readied for the endgame. The original idea was to make it appear that Sharon had taken her own life, but then Tanya changed her mind. Suicide was too easy, and could perhaps arouse some suspicion as well. Besides, she was brimming with the confidence of having executed perfectly a bold and intricate plan so far.

Tanya had already decided on the spot where she would stage the accident. It was at a sharp curve on the highway, next to a wide grassy verge that fell away into a deep ravine. It would be quite plausible that Sharon was under stress and driving fast, didn't see the curve in the darkness of the night, and crashed to her death six hundred feet below.

Unfortunately for Tanya, when she pushed the car, with Sharon in the driver's seat, the tree prevented it from rolling all the way down the steep hillside. She cursed and tried to back it up for another run, but the engine had been damaged in the collision and wouldn't start. The impact was nevertheless severe, and she saw that Sharon was badly injured. Tanya felt for her pulse but couldn't find one.

To be doubly sure, she took a rock and smashed it on Sharon's forehead before walking away.

EPILOGUE

THE duty nurse checked the IV drip and glanced at the monitor. The heart rate and blood pressure were both abnormally low. It was remarkable that the woman was still alive.

It was the nurse's first ICU roster, but he knew all about that particular patient. The Ocean West murders continued to fascinate the press and dominate social media. The striking face of Sharon Sequeira had been splashed all over, though the haggard, unconscious woman lying on the hospital bed looked nothing like that any more. Anyway, she would likely be out of her misery soon.

The nurse sighed. From all the facts of the case he had read, he felt sorry for Sharon. She seemed like a normal girl who had been driven by unfortunate circumstances to commit murder and was now being unfairly punished for it. He knew what it was like to be cheated upon. *If only I had her courage,* he thought.

He pushed aside the plastic curtain and was about to move on to the next patient when something made him turn around.

Sharon's eyes were *open.* She whispered faintly, 'Where… am I?'

www.ingramcontent.com/pod-product-compliance
Lightning Source LLC
La Vergne TN
LVHW100523110826
845146LV00002B/748

9789355439727